This book
belongs to:

_____

_____

365
Bedtime
Stories
and Rhymes

Original stories written by: Annie Baker, David Bedford, Peter Bently, Dawn Casey, Rachel Elliot, Claire Freedman, Lulu Frost, Timothy Knapman and Steve Smallman. Fairy tales and fables retold by Claire Sipi.

Cover illustrated by Birgitta Sif.
Illustrated by: Deborah Allwright, Victoria Assanelli, Barroux, Maria Bogade, Alison Brown, Lorna Brown, Fran Brylewska, Ying Fan Chen, Livia Coloji, Charlotte Cooke, Valeria Docampo, Jacqueline East, Rebecca Elliott, Nicola Evans, Emma Foster, Emma Levey, Polona Lovsin, Natalie Hinrichsen, Tamsin Hinrichsen, Katy Hudson, Russell Julian, Sean Julian, Dubravka Kolanovic, Deborah Melmon, Mei Matsuoka, Susie Poole, Alessandra Psacharopulo, Karen Sapp, Gavin Scott, Jaime Temairik, Brenna Vaughan, Erica-Jane Waters, Steve Whitlow and Gail Yerrill.

Every effort has been made to acknowledge the contributors to this book.
If we have made any errors, we will be pleased to rectify them in future editions.

365

Bedtime

Stories

and Rhymes

cottage
door
press

Contents

Goldilocks and the Three Bears

Once upon a time there was a little girl named Goldilocks who had beautiful golden hair. She lived in a little cottage right at the edge of the forest.

One morning, before breakfast, Goldilocks skipped into the forest to play. She soon strayed far from home and began to feel hungry.

Just as she was thinking about going home, a delicious smell wafted through the woods. She followed it all the way to a little cottage.

"I wonder who lives here?" thought Goldilocks. She knocked on the door, but there was no answer.

As Goldilocks pushed gently on the door, it swung open, and Goldilocks stepped inside.

The delicious smell was coming from three bowls of steaming porridge on a table. There was a great big bowl, a middle-sized bowl, and a teeny-tiny bowl.

Goldilocks was so hungry, she tried the porridge in the biggest bowl first.

"Ooh! Too hot," she cried.

Next she tasted the porridge in the middle-sized bowl.

"Yuck! Too cold," she spluttered.

So Goldilocks tried the porridge in the teeny-tiny bowl.

"Yum," she said. "Just right." And she ate it all up.

Goldilocks saw three comfy chairs by the fire. There was a great big chair, a middle-sized chair, and a teeny-tiny chair.

"Just the place for a nap," yawned Goldilocks sleepily.

She tried to scramble onto the biggest chair. "Too high up!" she gasped, sliding to the ground.

Next Goldilocks tried the middle-sized chair, but she sank into the cushions. "Too squishy!" she grumbled.

So Goldilocks tried the teeny-tiny chair. "Just right!" she sighed, settling down. But Goldilocks was full of porridge and too heavy for the teeny-tiny chair. It squeaked and creaked. Creaked and cracked. Then … CRASH!

It broke into teeny-tiny pieces, and Goldilocks fell to the floor.

"Ouch!" she said.

Goldilocks climbed up the stairs. At the top she found a bedroom with three beds. There was a great big bed, a middle-sized bed, and a teeny-tiny bed.

"I'll just lie down for a while," yawned Goldilocks. So she clambered onto the biggest bed. "Too hard," she grumbled.

Then she lay down on the middle-sized bed. "Too soft!" she mumbled.

So she snuggled down in the teeny-tiny bed. "Just right," she sighed, and fell fast asleep.

Meanwhile, a great big daddy bear, a middle-sized mommy bear, and a teeny-tiny baby bear returned home from their walk in the woods.

"The porridge should be cool enough to eat now," said Mommy Bear.

So the three bears went inside their cottage for breakfast.

"Someone's been eating my porridge," growled Daddy Bear, looking in his bowl.

"Someone's been eating my porridge," gasped Mommy Bear, looking in her bowl.

"Someone's been eating my porridge," squeaked Baby Bear, "and they've eaten it all up!"

Then Daddy Bear went over to his chair.

"Someone's been sitting in my chair," he roared. "There's a golden hair on it!'"

"Someone's been sitting in my chair," growled Mommy Bear. "The cushions are all squashed."

"Someone's been sitting in my chair," cried Baby Bear, "and they've broken it!"

The three bears stomped upstairs.

Daddy Bear looked at his crumpled bed covers.

"Someone's been sleeping in my bed!" he grumbled.

Mommy Bear looked at the jumbled pillows on her bed.

"Someone's been sleeping in my bed!" she said.

Baby Bear padded over to his bed.

"Someone's been sleeping in my bed," he cried, "and they're still there!"

At that moment, Goldilocks woke up. When she saw the three bears, she leaped out of the bed, ran down the stairs, through the door, into the woods, and all the way home! And she never visited the house of the three bears ever again.

Twinkle, Twinkle, Little Star

Twinkle, twinkle, little star,
How I wonder what you are!
Up above the world so high,
Like a diamond in the sky.

When the blazing sun is gone,
When he nothing shines upon,
Then you show your little light,
Twinkle, twinkle, all the night.

Bed in Summer

In winter I get up at night,
And dress by yellow candlelight.
In summer, quite the other way,
I have to go to bed by day.

Golden Slumbers

Golden slumbers kiss your eyes,
Smiles await you when you rise.
Sleep, pretty baby, do not cry,
And I will sing a lullaby.

Bedtime

The evening is coming; the sun sinks to rest,
The rooks are all flying straight home to nest.
"Caw!' says the rook, as he flies overhead;
"It's time little people were going to bed!"

Red Sky at Night

Red sky at night, shepherd's delight.
Red sky in the morning, shepherd's warning.

Now the Day Is Over

Now the day is over,
Night is drawing nigh,
Shadows of the evening
Steal across the sky.

Now the darkness gathers,
Stars begins to peep,
Birds and beasts and flowers
Soon will be asleep.

Troll Two ... Three ... Four ...

Trolls like to laze about twiddling their toes,
Picking their noses, and having a doze.
They love to creep up behind goats and go, "Boo!"
Except for one sad, lonely troll: Boogaloo.

The other trolls tried but could not understand
Why Boogaloo felt so alone in Troll Land.
"All I want is a friend," he thought with a sigh,
And just then, a shiny red THING floated by!

He ran after the thing and was running so fast,
He went straight by the sign that
no troll should go past!

A second troll followed behind Boogaloo,
Thinking, "Where is he going? I want to go too!"
They walked through the Keep-out Clouds straight to a place
Where a human being stood with a very shocked face.

The human being screamed, "I SEE TROLLS!" very loud,
And fled as a third troll came out of the cloud.
Another troll—number four—followed them too,
Marching in line right behind Boogaloo.

And before you could say "boogie-boo!" there were crowds
Of curious trolls popping out through the clouds.
Trolls filthy and furry were marching along,
Singing their favorite troll marching song …

"Troll, two, three, four … we're the trolls who grunt and snore.
Troll, two, three, four … we don't know, there might be more,
But we can only count to four!"

The humans were frightened—the trolls looked so scary,
So scruffy and smelly, so horrid and hairy!
As the trolls passed a park, Boogaloo sneaked away.
He opened the gate and ran in to play!

In a house just nearby, a boy stood on a chair.
He whispered, "Hey, look, there's a troll over there!
He looks a bit lonely, I'll just go and see
If maybe he'd play with somebody like me."

"Hello," said the boy, "my name's Jake. Who are you?"
The little troll smiled and said, "Boogaloo!"
"Come play on this whiz-thing!" Boogaloo cried.
"All right," answered Jake. "But we call it a slide."

"Will you be my very best friend, Boogaloo?"
"Yes please!" the troll answered. "Will you be mine too?"
And humans and trolls all crept closer to see
What very best friends trolls and humans could be.

There is nothing between trolls and humans today:
The signs all came down, the clouds drifted away.
Together they play with balloons and toy boats,
And no one is frightened … not even the goats!

The Little Red Hen

There was once a little red hen who lived on a farm with her friends: a sleepy cat, a lazy pig, and a stuck-up duck.

One day, the little red hen found some grains of wheat.

"If I plant these," she thought, "they will grow tall and strong and make more wheat!"

She went to see her friends.

"Who will help me plant these grains of wheat?" she asked.

"Not I," mewed the cat.

"Not I," snorted the pig.

"Not I," quacked the duck.

So the little red hen planted the grains of wheat, and tended to the growing wheat all summer. At last, the wheat was ready to harvest.

"Who will help me harvest the wheat?" the little red hen asked her friends.

"Not I," mewed the cat.

"Not I," snorted the pig.

"Not I," quacked the duck.

So the little red hen harvested the wheat, then went back to her friends.

"Who will help me carry the harvested wheat to the mill?" she asked.

"Not I," mewed the cat.

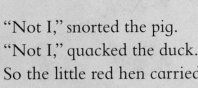

"Not I," snorted the pig.

"Not I," quacked the duck.

So the little red hen carried the heavy sack of wheat to the mill, where the kind miller ground it to flour.

"Who will help me bake a loaf of bread with this flour?" she asked.

"Not I," mewed the cat.

"Not I," snorted the pig.

"Not I," quacked the duck.

So the little red hen baked a loaf of bread all by herself. "Who will help me eat this delicious bread?" the little red hen asked quietly.

"I will!" mewed the cat.

"I will!" snorted the pig.

"I will!" quacked the duck.

"No, you will not!" cried the little red hen. "I did all the work, and no one helped. My chicks and I will eat the loaf!"

And the little red hen and her little chicks ate up every crumb of the hot, fresh bread.

Counting Stars

Tomorrow was Little Panda's first day at school, and she was very excited. Daddy tucked her in her bed, but she was too wide-awake to close her eyes.

"I wonder what new friends I'll meet?" she said. "I can't wait to find my desk and meet my teacher. School is going to be so much fun!"

Daddy tried to make Little Panda feel sleepy. He read stories, he sang lullabies, and he stroked her soft fur, but she was still wide awake.

"All right," he said. "Whatever you do, don't go to sleep. You must stay awake until you have counted every single star in the sky."

The sky was crowded with twinkling stars. Little Panda started to count them.

"One … two … three … four …"

Before she even reached number ten, Little Panda's eyelids had drooped and she'd fallen fast asleep. And what did she dream about? Her first day at school, of course!

Lion's First Day

It was clumsy Lion's first day at Miss Giraffe's Savanna School. True to his nature, he arrived late, skidded into the classroom, tripped over his paws, and landed upside down in his chair.

Miss Giraffe tilted her head and smiled kindly at Lion.

"What an amazing acrobat you are!" she said.

At lunchtime, Lion bumped into the table and knocked all the food over. Then he spilled his drink and slipped across the floor.

"What wonderful clown skills you have!" said Miss Giraffe.

At playtime, Lion tripped and knocked some balls off a shelf, catching three with his paws and one on the tip of his tail.

"What a fantastic juggler you'd make!" said Miss Giraffe.

That evening, Lion couldn't wait to tell his mother about his day.

"All this time I thought I was clumsy, but Miss Giraffe thinks I'm an acrobat!" he said. "And a clown and a juggler!"

His mother smiled.

"You can be a magician, too—just make your dinner disappear!"

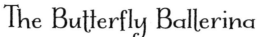

The Butterfly Ballerina

Isabella Ballerina loved ballet. Best of all, she liked going to Madame Colette's Ballet School.

"Let us practice our ballet positions!" called Madame Colette one morning, clapping her hands. "No, no, Isabella! You are pointing the wrong foot again!"

"Sorry!" Isabella said. "I'm always getting my left and right mixed up!"

"Now, girls," cried Madame Colette. "I have exciting news to announce! We will be putting on our first show, the Butterfly Ballet. I will choose girls to play raindrop butterflies and rainbow butterflies, and one girl to dance as the sunshine butterfly!"

Back home, Isabella told Mom all about the ballet show.

"I just wish I could remember my left from my right!" she sighed.

Mom smiled. "This might help." She gave Isabella a beautiful butterfly bracelet. "Wear it on your right wrist. Then you'll always be able to tell which way is right."

At each ballet lesson, Isabella kept looking at her butterfly bracelet to make sure she turned the right way!

Finally, after many rehearsals, Madame Colette told the girls their roles.

"Isabella, you shall play the sunshine butterfly. As you twirl so beautifully, you will dance the final pirouette!" said Madame Colette.

Isabella smiled. She just hoped she would turn the right way!

The week before the show, Isabella practiced her pirouettes everywhere! She twirled in the garden … in her bedroom … and at the park.

On the night of the big show, all the girls dressed in tutus and shimmering butterfly wings. The lights dimmed. Beautiful music filled the room. The ballet was about to begin!

The raindrop and rainbow butterflies danced gracefully from flower to flower.

At last it was Isabella's turn to dance. Nervously, she touched her butterfly bracelet. Then, taking a deep breath, she twirled the most perfect pirouette she had ever twirled!

The girls joined Isabella on stage, and they all curtsied.

"Oops!" giggled Isabella. She had curtsied with the wrong foot forward, but it didn't matter one little bit.

She would always be Isabella, Butterfly Ballerina!

Oranges and Lemons

Oranges and lemons,
Say the bells of St. Clement's.
You owe me five farthings,
Say the bells of St. Martin's.
When will you pay me?
Say the bells of Old Bailey.
When I grow rich,
Say the bells of Shoreditch.

Boys and Girls Come Out to Play

Boys and girls, come out to play,
The moon does shine as bright as day!
Leave your supper, and leave your sleep,
And join your playfellows in the street.
Come with a whoop, and come with a call,
Come with a good will or not at all.

How the Leopard Got Its Spots

Long ago, Leopard lived on a sandy-yellow plain in Africa. Giraffes and zebras and deer lived there too. The animals were sandy-yellow all over, just like the plain itself. Leopard was sandy-yellow, too, which wasn't good for the rest of the animals because he could hide in the sandy-yellow grasses, then jump out and eat them.

After a while the other animals had had enough. They decided to move away from the sandy plain into the forest. In the forest, the sun shone through the trees, making stripy, spotty, and patchy shadows on the ground.

The animals hid themselves there, and while they hid their skins changed color, becoming stripy, spotty, and patchy too.

Meanwhile, Leopard was hungry.

"Where has everyone gone?" he asked Baboon.

"To the forest," said Baboon carelessly, "to hide from you!"

Leopard decided to go to the forest to hunt for his dinner. But when he got there, all he could see were tree trunks. They were stripy, spotty, and patchy with shadows. He couldn't see the other animals, but he could smell them so he knew they were there.

Meanwhile, the other animals could easily spot the sandy-yellow leopard in the forest, so they stayed hidden away.

Hungry and tired, Leopard lay down in a spotty shadow to rest. After a while, he noticed he wasn't sandy-yellow any more. He had small, dark spots on his skin just like the spotty shadow he was lying in.

"A-ha!" he thought. "Giraffe and Zebra and the other animals must have changed skin color too. But now that my skin is no longer sandy-yellow, I can hide too. Then, when they come close, I can leap out and eat them up."

With that, the spotty leopard set off into the shadowy forest to eat, sleep, and NOT be spotted. And the other animals learned to hide from him as best they could, too!

You're a Big Sister

You're going to be a big sister!
And that's so lucky for you …
Babies LOVE their big sisters
And the clever things that they do.

Big sisters know babies like quiet,
So just smile and whisper, "Hello."
Big sisters are really good helpers.
Let's all get ready … and go!

All babies are cute … fun … and cuddly,
But there are things a big sister soon knows …
Babies dribble … kick …
And might even be sick …
All over your clothes and your toes!

Though they are so very tiny,
Babies can make a BIG STINK …
And when they're not feeling well …
Babies scream … and yell …
So loud you can't hear yourself think!

Babies haven't learned to play fair yet.
But remember, you were little once too!
So be kind and share …
Cuddle, play, and take care …
And help them be clever like you!

When Mommy and Daddy are busy,
Always know that they love you too …
And now that you're a big sister,
Enjoy sharing with somebody new!

31

Little Bo-Peep

Little Bo-Peep has lost her sheep
And doesn't know where to find them.
Leave them alone
And they'll come home,
Wagging their tails behind them.

Miss Mary Mack

Miss Mary Mack, all dressed in black,
With silver buttons all down her back,
She asked her mother for fifty cents,
To see the elephant jump the fence,
He jumped so high, he touched the sky,
And didn't come back till the Fourth of July.

Baa, Baa, Black Sheep

Baa, baa, black sheep,
Have you any wool?
Yes sir, yes sir,
Three bags full.

One for the master,
And one for the dame,
And one for the little boy
Who lives down the lane.

Sippity Sup, Sippity Sup

Sippity sup, sippity sup,
Bread and milk from a china cup.
Bread and milk from a bright silver spoon
Made of a piece of the bright silver moon.
Sippity sup, sippity sup,
Sippity, sippity sup.

Star Light, Star Bright

Star light, star bright,
The first star I see tonight;
I wish I may, I wish I might,
Have the wish I wish tonight.

Hey Diddle Diddle

Hey diddle diddle,
The cat and the fiddle,
The cow jumped over the moon.
The little dog laughed to see such sport
And the dish ran away with the spoon!

Want to Swap?

It was bedtime, but Duck couldn't sleep. "I'm bored being a duck and nibbling waterweeds," she said to herself.

Then she saw her friend Rooster strolling around the pond and had a brilliant idea.

"Hey, Rooster," she called. "Want to swap jobs?"

"Okay," Rooster agreed. "Nibbling waterweeds is better than getting up early every day."

So the next morning, Duck waddled to the farmhouse for her first cock-a-doodle-do to wake the farmer up. But when she opened her beak …

"Quack! Quack! QUACK!"

Poor Duck! However hard she tried, she couldn't crow, and the farmer overslept.

"I want my old job back," Duck said sadly.

Luckily for Duck, Rooster was not enjoying his new job much either.

"Waterweeds are yucky, and I kind of missed waking the farmer up," he said.

The next day, when Duck saw Sheepdog herding sheep, she had a thought. She waddled up to the field.

"That looks like fun, Sheepdog," she said. "Want to swap?"

Sheep's Bad Mood

Sheep was in a bad mood. His friends on the farm tried to cheer him up, but their jokes didn't help. Sheep just felt as if there was a growly bear inside him trying to get out.

"I've an idea," said Horse, who was very clever about this sort of thing. "Try doing some hard work."

"How can hard work help?" Sheep grumbled. But no one had any better ideas, so Sheep decided to give it a try. He carried baskets of eggs for the chickens. He lifted bales of hay for the horses. He rode in the tractor with the farmer. He worked so hard that he started to forget about his bad mood. And at bedtime, when all the weary farm animals snuggled down in the barn, Horse noticed that Sheep was smiling.

"Has it gone?" asked Horse.

"Has what gone?" yawned Sheep.

"Your bad mood," said Horse, chuckling loudly.

But there was no reply. Sheep was already fast asleep!

Captain Rustybeard's New Rules

Captain Rustybeard loved being a pirate … mostly. "I just wish there weren't so many rules," he grumbled, thumping the Pirate Rulebook. He didn't seem to be allowed to do any of the things he really wanted.

"I'd like a pet dog," Captain Rustybeard said one day.

"Pirates don't have dogs," said the first mate, looking astonished. "A parrot is the only pet for a pirate captain. Look in the rulebook."

"My feet ache," said Captain Rustybeard another day. "I think I'll get myself a nice, comfy pair of slippers."

"Pirates don't wear slippers!" said the boatswain in a shocked voice. "They wear stiff leather boots. It's rule number five."

"But leather boots give me blisters," Captain Rustybeard grumbled.

One sunny afternoon, Captain Rustybeard looked down through the clear water and saw dozens of oyster shells on the seabed.

"Let's dive for pearls!" he cried.

"Pirates don't dive for pearls," said the cabin boy with a gasp. "We're supposed to rob them from other ships. Do you know the Pirate Rulebook at all?"

Captain Rustybeard flung the rulebook down on the deck and jumped up and down on it.

"I'm tired of being told what pirates don't do!" he roared. "From now on, I'm going to decide on the rules!"

At first, the members of the crew were worried. What if other pirates laughed at them? But after a while, they started to enjoy themselves. After all, sheepskin slippers were a lot cozier than leather boots. The Captain's pet dog knew some good tricks, and they found more pearls by diving for them than by robbing ships.

"This is the life for me!" exclaimed Captain Rustybeard, wiggling his toes in his new slippers.

Soon, every pirate on the high seas had heard about Captain Rustybeard's new rules, and can you guess what?

They all wanted to join his crew!

Old King Cole

Old King Cole was a merry old soul
And a merry old soul was he.
He called for his pipe, and he called for his bowl,
And he called for his fiddlers three.
Every fiddler had a very fine fiddle
And a very fine fiddle had he.
Oh there's none so rare as can compare,
With King Cole and his fiddlers three.

Hector Protector

Hector Protector was dressed all in green;
Hector Protector was sent to the Queen.
The Queen did not like him,
No more did the King;
So Hector Protector was sent back again.

The Grand
Old Duke of York

The grand old Duke of York,
He had ten thousand men.
He marched them up to the top of the hill
And he marched them down again.
When they were up, they were up.
And when they were down, they were down.
And when they were only halfway up,
They were neither up nor down.

Ring Around the Rosie

Ring around the rosie,
A pocket full of posies.
Ashes, ashes,
We all fall down!

Scaredy Boo

Under the bed lived a monster,
A monster named Scaredy Boo.
Boo was afraid of everything.
He would have been scared of you!

Each night, the other small monsters
Raced around the house having fun.
Though all the children were sleeping,
Boo feared they'd wake up someone!

Boo sighed, "I'm frightened of Big Things.
Small Things and Wiggly Things too!
I'm little Scaredy Boo monster.
Wouldn't these things scare you?"

Scaredy Boo didn't like noises,
Things that went crackle or squeak.
Hearing strange whispers and rustles
Made poor Boo's legs get all weak!

Late one night, Boo heard loud footsteps.
"Help! Something's out there!" he said.
"Hello," the Thing called. "You hiding?"
It peeked at Boo under the bed.

Scaredy Boo trembled. "Who are you?
I jump when someone shouts BOO!
I'm little Scaredy Boo monster.
Wouldn't you be scared too?"

"Why are you scared?" smiled the stranger.
"I'm Spike—a monster like you!
Come out, and let's play together.
Playing's what monsters do!"

Poor Boo felt ever so worried.
He'd never been out before.
Night-time was all dark and scary!
Creakity-creak, creaked the floor.

"Come on!" Spike called to Boo kindly.
"Let's play with all of these toys!"
"Shh!" Scaredy whispered. "The children!
You'll wake them with all of the noise!"

Boo saw a huge black shape looming!
Oh, what a horrible sight!
"Help!" he cried, diving for cover.
There he sat, shaking with fright.

Scaredy Boo stuttered, "Wh-hat is that?
I jump when someone shouts BOO!
I'm little Scaredy Boo monster.
Wouldn't you be scared too?"

"That's just your shadow!" Spike told Boo.
"Everything has one—look, see?"
Scaredy Boo felt a little bit silly:
"All I was scared of was me!"

"Help! There's a Twitchy Thing!" Boo gasped.
Spike grinned, "It's only a mouse!"
"Oooh! It's quite friendly!" Boo giggled.
"I like exploring this house!"

Scaredy Boo met all of the monsters.
"It's so much fun playing," he said.
"Thank you, Spike—I'm glad you found me.
It's lonely under the bed!"

Wheee! From a shelf dropped a spider.
Scaredy Boo's fur stood on end!
"I still don't like spiders!" Boo giggled.
"They scare me too!" laughed his friend.

Boo shouted, "Let's play tomorrow!
It's so exciting and new!"
"Shh!" all his monster friends whispered.
"YOU'RE noisy now, little Boo!"

Arabella Miller

Little Arabella Miller found a hairy caterpillar.
First it crawled upon her mother,
Then upon her baby brother.
All said: "Arabella Miller, take away that caterpillar!"

Oats and Beans and Barley Grow

Oats and beans and barley grow,
Oats and beans and barley grow.
Do you or I or anyone know
How oats and beans and barley grow?

First the farmer sows his seed,
Then he stands and takes his ease.
He stamps his feet and claps his hands
And turns around to view the lands.

Each Peach, Pear, Plum

Each peach, pear, plum, out goes Tom Thumb;
Tom Thumb won't do, out goes Betty Blue;
Betty Blue won't go, so out goes you.

Peter, Peter

Peter, Peter, pumpkin eater,
Had a wife and couldn't keep her.
He put her in a pumpkin shell,
And there he kept her very well.

Monday's Child

Monday's child is fair of face,
Tuesday's child is full of grace,
Wednesday's child is full of woe,
Thursday's child has far to go,
Friday's child is loving and giving,
Saturday's child works hard for his living,
And the child that is born on the Sabbath day
Is fair and wise and good and gay.

Lavender's Blue

Lavender's blue, dilly, dilly,
Lavender's green;
When I am king, dilly, dilly,
You shall be queen.

The Party Zoo

E very evening, the zookeeper closed up the zoo for the night and went to bed in his zookeeper's hut. And every night there was peace and quiet in the zoo … except tonight.

"Let's have a party!" said Monkey, just as the zookeeper had gone to bed.

All the other animals thought it was a wonderful idea.

"There's a lot to organize!" said Monkey, feeling excited.

Everyone had an important job to do. The baboon band practiced their music, and the penguins made iced drinks. At last, the party could begin. And WHAT a party it was!

The penguins and the dolphins had a belly-flop competition and drenched the leopards next door. Monkey fired party poppers as he swung through the trees, and the giraffe danced to the baboon band's music. The music got louder … and louder … and louder … until it woke the zookeeper up!

eyes. The ostrich was doing the hokey-pokey with the hippo, and the tigers and the lions were playing pass the parcel.

"I must be dreaming!" said the zookeeper. "It's a very good dream—I hope I don't wake up!"

Then he hurried back to bed as fast as he could.

In the morning, the zoo was very quiet. All the animals were still asleep after the party. The zookeeper thought about his dream as he swept the paths, and then he saw something lying under the tree where Monkey was going to sleep. It was a party popper!

"If I didn't know better, I'd think my dream was real!" chuckled the zookeeper.

And as he drifted off to sleep, Monkey smiled a mischievous little smile.

47

The Wheels on the Bus

The wheels on the bus go
round and round!
Round and round!
Round and round!
The wheels on the bus go
round and round!
All day long.

Now sing it again, substituting the different parts of the bus and
what they do: wipers (swish), horn (beep), people (up and down).

Ten in the Bed

There were ten in the bed and the little one said,
"Roll over, roll over."
So they all rolled over and one fell out.

There were nine in the bed and the little one said,
"Roll over, roll over."
So they all rolled over and one fell out.

There were eight in the bed and the little one said,
"Roll over, roll over."
So they all rolled over and one fell out.

*(Repeat the rhyme, counting down from seven in the bed
to one in the bed ...)*

There was one in the bed and the little one said,
"Goodnight!"

49

Puss in Boots

There was once an old miller who had three sons. When the miller died, he left the mill to his oldest son. The middle son was given the donkeys. The youngest son, a kind man who had always put his father and brothers before himself, was left nothing but his father's cat.

"What will become of me?" sighed the young miller's son, looking at his cat.

"Buy me a fine pair of boots and I will help you make your fortune, just as your father had wished," replied the cat.

A talking cat! The miller's son could not believe his ears.

He bought the cat a fine pair of boots, and the two of them set off to seek their fortune.

After a while they came to a grand palace.

"I wish I could live so grandly," sighed the miller's son.

Later, the cat went hunting and caught a rabbit. He put it in a sack and took it to the king.

"A gift from my master, the Marquis of Carabas," said the cat, pretending the miller's son was a grand nobleman.

"Now the king will want to know all about you," laughed the cat, when he told his master what he had done.

The cat delivered gifts all that week, and the king became very curious. So much so, he decided his daughter should meet this mysterious Marquis of Carabas.

The clever cat rushed back to his master, telling him to take off all his clothes and stand in the river by the side of the road.

The puzzled miller's son did as he was told, and the cat quickly hid his master's tattered clothes behind a rock.

When the cat heard the king's carriage coming, he jumped out into the road.

"Your majesty," cried the cat, "my master's clothes were stolen while he was bathing in the river."

The king gave the miller's son a suit of fine clothes to wear and invited him into the carriage.

The miller's son looked very handsome in his new suit, and the king's daughter fell in love with him at once.

Meanwhile, the cat quickly ran on ahead. Every time he met people working in the fields, he told them, "If the king stops to ask who owns this land, you must tell him it belongs to the Marquis of Carabas."

Beyond the fields, the cat reached a grand castle belonging to a fierce ogre. The cat bravely knocked on the door and called out: "I have heard that you are a very clever ogre, and I would like to see what tricks you can do."

The ogre, who liked to show off his tricks, immediately changed himself into a snarling lion.

"Very clever," said the cat, "but a lion is large, and I think it would be more impressive to change into a tiny mouse."

At once the ogre changed into a little mouse, and the cat pounced on him and ate him up!

Then the cat went into the castle. He told all the servants that their new master was the Marquis of Carabas, and that the king was coming to visit them.

When the king arrived at the castle, the cat purred, "Your majesty, welcome to the home of the Marquis of Carabas."

The cunning cat told his master to ask the king for his daughter's hand in marriage. And that's what he did!

The king, impressed by the nobleman's wealth, agreed, and soon the Marquis of Carabas and the princess were married.

The cat was made a lord of their court and was given the most splendid clothes, which he wore proudly with his fine boots. And they all lived happily ever after.

What's in a Name?

One morning, Tailorbird was busy fluttering this way and that around the forest when a little mongoose called out to her from the ground.

"Why are you called Tailorbird?" asked Mongoose.

"I'm very sorry, but I'm too busy to talk," chirped Tailorbird. "You'll just have to wait and see."

So the mongoose sat down to watch. First Tailorbird used her sharp beak to pierce tiny holes in two big leaves. Then she threaded a long piece of spider's silk through the holes to join the leaves together. Next she lined the cradle of leaves with soft wool to make it warm and cozy.

When she was finished, she poked her head out of her new nest.

"Now you know why I'm called Tailorbird," she chirped.

"Yes, I do," Mongoose laughed. "It's because you are so good at sewing, just like a tailor who makes clothes … but you create wonderful nests instead!"

Little Sheep

Little Sheep couldn't sleep,
Not a wink, not a peep!
Tossing, turning, all night through,
What was poor Little Sheep to do?

Owl came by, old and wise,
Said, "Silly sheep, use your eyes—
You're lying in a field of sheep,
Try counting them to help you sleep!"

"Seven, four, thirteen, ten—
That's not right, I'll start again …"
Till daylight came, awake he lay
And vowed he'd learn to count next day!

Old MacDonald Had a Farm

Old MacDonald had a farm,
Ee-i-ee-i-o!
And on that farm he had a cow,
Ee-i-ee-i-o!
With a moo-moo here,
And a moo-moo there,
Here a moo, there a moo,
Everywhere a moo-moo,
Old MacDonald had a farm,
Ee-i-ee-i-o!

Now sing it again, using these animals and their sounds:
Sheep (baa), horse (neigh), pig (oink), duck (quack).

Ip Dip

Ip dip, sky blue.
Who's it? Not you.
Not because you're dirty,
Not because you're clean,
My mother says you're the fairy queen.

Little Squirrel

Nibble, nibble, little squirrel,
Nibble nuts for tea.
Scamper, scamper, little squirrel,
Scamper up a tree.

Tom, Tom, the Piper's Son

Tom, Tom, the piper's son,
Stole a pig and away did run.
The pig was eat, and Tom was beat,
And Tom went crying down the street.

Underpants Thunderpants

One day when the weather is sunny and fine,
Dog hangs his underpants out on the line.
But thunder and lightning soon fill up the sky.
Underpants Thunderpants!
Look at them fly!
Over the ocean, the jungle and town—
Where will those undies come fluttering down?

58

"How odd," says the submarine captain below.
"First I saw lightning and now I see snow!"
Octopus wriggles and jiggles with glee.
"Four pairs of underpants perfect for me!"

Underpants Plunderpants!
Just imagine that!
Roger the Pirate has got a new hat!

Elephant's trunk has been tickled by bees.
"Oh bother!" he grumbles. "I'm going to sneeze,
But I don't have a tissue. What shall I do?
A jumbo-sized hankie! How handy!
ACHOO!"

Watch it! A hunter is out on the snoop.
Underpants Blunderpants!
Splat in the poop!

60

Up at the palace, the king says,
"Oh my! Three pairs of underpants
baked in a pie!"

A two-headed alien stares from his lair …
"Underpants Wonderpants!
Now I'm not bare!"

Mary, Mary, Quite Contrary

Mary, Mary, quite contrary,
How does your garden grow?
With silver bells and cockle shells
And pretty maids all in a row.

Slowly, Slowly

Slowly, slowly, very slowly,
Creeps the garden snail.
Slowly, slowly, very slowly,
Up the wooden rail.

Quickly, quickly, very quickly,
Runs the little mouse.
Quickly, quickly, very quickly,
Round about the house.

Solomon Grundy

Solomon Grundy,
Born on a Monday,
Christened on Tuesday,
Married on Wednesday,
Took ill on Thursday,
Grew worse on Friday,
Died on Saturday,
Buried on Sunday.
That was the end of
Solomon Grundy.

One, Two, Buckle My Shoe

One, two, buckle my shoe,
Three, four, knock at the door,
Five, six, pick up sticks,
Seven, eight, lay them straight,
Nine, ten, a big fat hen,
Eleven, twelve, dig and delve,
Thirteen, fourteen, maids a-courting,
Fifteen, sixteen, maids in the kitchen,
Seventeen, eighteen, maids in waiting,
Nineteen, twenty, my plate's empty!

One Potato, Two Potato

One potato, two potato,
Three potato, four.
Five potato, six potato,
Seven potato,
MORE!

Eeny, Meeny

Eeny, meeny, miny, moe,
Catch a tiger by the toe,
If he hollers, let him go,
Eeny, meeny, miny, moe.

How the Bear Lost His Tail

Once upon a time, the bear had a long tail, and the fox was very jealous of it.

"What makes Bear think his tail is so wonderful?" growled the fox, as he looked at his own splendid russet-colored tail. "My tail is much finer than his. I'm going to teach him a lesson."

It was winter, and all the lakes were covered with thick ice. The fox made a hole in the ice and surrounded it with fat, tasty-looking fish. That evening, when the bear passed by, the fox dangled his tail through the hole into the water.

"What are you doing?" the bear asked.

"I am fishing," the fox replied. "Would you like to try?"

The bear loved fish, so he was very eager to try.

"This is what you must do," the crafty fox explained. "Put your lovely long tail in the hole. Soon a fish will grab it, and then you can pull the fish out. In the meantime, you must be very patient and stay perfectly still."

The bear was hungry and wanted to catch some fish, so he did exactly as the fox had told him.

The next morning, the fox went back to the lake and saw that the bear was lying on the ice. He was fast asleep and covered with snow. The hole had frozen over during the night, and now the bear's tail was trapped in the ice.

The fox called out, "You've caught a fish! Quick! Pull out your tail!"

The bear woke up with a start and tugged his tail as hard as he could. All of a sudden, there was a loud CRACK! as the bear's frozen tail snapped off.

And that explains why bears now have very short tails and why they are definitely not friends with foxes!

Eat, Birds, Eat!

Eat, birds, eat, and make no waste;
I lie here, and make no haste:
If my master chance to come,
You must fly, and I must run!

Once I Saw a Little Bird

Once I saw a little bird
Come hop, hop, hop;
So I cried, "Little bird,
Will you stop, stop, stop?"
I was going to the window,
To say, "How do you do?"
But he shook his little tail,
And far away he flew.

The Little Bird

This little bird flaps its wings,
Flaps its wings, flaps its wings,
This little bird flaps its wings,
And flies away in the morning!

Coffee and Tea

Molly, my sister, and I fell out,
And what do you think it was all about?
She loved coffee and I loved tea,
And that was the reason we couldn't agree.

Polly, Put the Kettle On

Polly, put the kettle on,
Polly, put the kettle on,
Polly, put the kettle on,
   We'll all have tea.

Sukey, take it off again,
Sukey, take it off again,
Sukey, take it off again,
   They've all gone away.

I'm a Little Teapot

I'm a little teapot, short and stout,
Here is my handle, here is my spout.
When I get all steamed up, hear me shout,
   Tip me over and pour me out.

You're a Big Brother

You're going to be a big brother!
Hooray! How lucky are you?
Babies love their big brothers
And the clever things that they do.

Babies are funny and friendly,
But there are things a big brother soon knows …
Babies can smell …
And pull hair as well …
So watch out and hold on to your nose!

Babies make moms and dads busy—
They won't just be caring for you.
But now that you're a big brother,
It's fun sharing with somebody new.

Babies don't do much to start with,
So just quietly show them your toys.
They can't dance or sing,
But they like to join in …
By making a gurgling noise!

Babies learn lots from big brothers,
So teach them all you can do:
Share and take care …
Be baby's best friend,
And they'll be amazing like YOU!

Cinderella

Once upon a time, there was a young girl who lived with her father, stepmother, and two stepsisters. The stepmother was unkind, and the stepsisters were mean. They made the girl do all the housework, eat scraps, and sleep by the fireplace among the cinders and ashes. Because she was always covered with cinders, they named her "Cinderella."

One morning, a special invitation arrived. All the young women in the kingdom were invited to a royal ball—a ball for the prince to choose a bride!

Cinderella longed to go, but her stepsisters just laughed.

"You? Go to a ball? In those rags? How ridiculous!" they cackled.

Instead, Cinderella had to rush around helping her stepsisters get ready for the ball.

As they left for the palace, Cinderella sat beside the fireplace and wept.

"I wish I could go to the ball," she cried.

Suddenly, a sparkle of light filled the dull kitchen, and there was—a fairy!

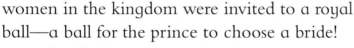

"Don't be afraid, my dear," she said. "I am your fairy godmother, and you SHALL go to the ball!"

"But how?" said Cinderella.

"Find me a big pumpkin, four white mice, and a rat," replied the fairy godmother.

Cinderella found everything as quickly as she could. The fairy godmother waved her wand, and the pumpkin changed into a magnificent golden coach, the white mice became white horses, and the rat became a coachman.

With one last gentle tap of her wand, the fairy godmother changed Cinderella's dusty dress into a shimmering ball gown. On her feet were two sparkling glass slippers.

"Now, off you go," said the fairy godmother, "but remember, all this will vanish at midnight, so make sure you are home by then."

Cinderella climbed into the coach, and it whisked her away to the palace.

Everyone was enchanted by the lovely stranger, especially the prince, who danced with her all evening. As Cinderella whirled around the room in his arms, she felt so happy that she completely forgot her fairy godmother's warning.

Suddenly, she heard the clock strike midnight …

BONG … BONG … BONG …

Cinderella picked up her
skirt and fled from the ballroom.
The worried prince ran after her.

BONG … BONG … BONG …
She ran down the palace steps, losing
a glass slipper on the way,
but she didn't dare stop.

BONG … BONG … BONG …
Cinderella jumped into
the coach, and it drove
off before he could stop her.

BONG … BONG … BONG!
On the final stroke of midnight,
Cinderella found herself sitting on the road beside a pumpkin,
four white mice, and a black rat. She was dressed in rags and
had only a single glass slipper left from her magical evening.

At the palace, the prince saw something twinkling on the
steps—a single glass slipper.

"I will marry the woman whose foot fits this glass slipper,"
he declared.

The next day, the prince took the glass slipper and visited
every house in the kingdom.

At last, the prince came to Cinderella's house. Her stepsisters tried and tried to squeeze their huge feet into the delicate slipper, but no matter what they did, they could not get the slipper to fit. Cinderella watched as she scrubbed the floor.

"May I try, please?" she asked.

"You didn't even go to the ball!" laughed the eldest stepsister.

"Everyone may try," said the prince, as he held out the sparkling slipper. And suddenly …

"Oh!" gasped the stepsisters, as Cinderella's dainty foot slipped easily into it.

The prince joyfully took Cinderella in his arms.

"Will you marry me?" he asked.

"I will!" Cinderella said.

Much to the disgust of her stepmother and stepsisters, soon Cinderella and the prince were married.

They lived long, happy lives together, and Cinderella's stepmother and stepsisters had to do their own cleaning and never went to a royal ball again.

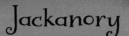

Jackanory

I'll tell you a story
Of Jackanory,
And now my story's begun;
I'll tell you another
Of Jack and his brother,
And now my story's done.

Three Wise Men of Gotham

Three wise men of Gotham
Went to sea in a bowl:
And if the bowl had been stronger,
My song would have been longer.

Little Tommy Tittlemouse

Little Tommy Tittlemouse,
Lived in a little house;
He caught fishes
In other men's ditches.

Aiken Drum

There was a man who lived on the moon,
Lived on the moon, lived on the moon.
There was a man who lived on the moon,
And his name was Aiken Drum.

Harry Parry

O rare Harry Parry,
When will you marry?
When apples and pears are ripe.
I'll come to your wedding,
Without any bidding,
And dance and sing all the night.

Lucy Locket

Lucy Locket lost her pocket,
Kitty Fisher found it.
Not a penny was there in it,
Only a ribbon round it.

Pink Is for Princesses

Princess Ava didn't like pink, which was a problem, because every single thing that anybody ever gave her was pink. Her bedroom was pink. Her clothes were pink. Even her hairbrush was pink. And one day, she decided that enough was enough.

"No more pink!" said Princess Ava in her firmest voice.

"Don't be silly," said her father, the king. "Pink is the best color for a princess."

"But I want to wear red and green and blue and purple!" Princess Ava pleaded.

The king shook his head.

"I won't allow it," he said stubbornly.

But Princess Ava was even more stubborn than her father. She put on her pink cloak, pulled her pink hood up so no one could recognize her, and marched off to the market. There were lots of stalls selling clothes and shoes and blankets and trinkets and balls of string in every color that she could imagine.

Princess Ava bought sky blue and grass-green gowns. She picked out white and blue shoes. She chose golden blankets and deep blue curtains.

"Who is that girl?" whispered the market sellers.

Back at the palace, Princess Ava collected up everything pink to be given away, and filled her room with every other color of the rainbow.

When the king saw Princess Ava's room, his eyes nearly popped out of his head. But then he looked at his daughter's big smile, and he smiled too.

"You were right," he said. "I'm sorry. These bright colors are perfect for you, and I love to see you looking happy."

And from that day on, no one gave Princess Ava anything pink ever again!

The Ant and the Dove

One morning, a thirsty ant went down to the river for a drink. Suddenly … SWOOSH! A ripple swept the tiny ant off the riverbank and into the water.

"Help!" cried the ant.

A kind dove heard the ant's cries. She swooped down and dropped a leaf into the water near him.

"Climb onto this," she cooed.

"Oh, thank you," gasped the ant. "You saved my life!" And he floated back to the shore on the leaf.

A little later, the ant was drying off in the sun when he saw a hunter trying to catch the dove with a net.

The ant wanted to help his new friend, so he scurried over to the hunter and bit his foot.

"Ouch!" yelled the hunter.

Startled by the noise, the dove flew away.

"Thank you," she called out to the ant. "Now you've saved my life, too!"

And the moral of the story is: One good turn deserves another.

The Fox and Grapes

One hot summer's day, a fox was walking through a field when he saw a bunch of grapes dangling high above his head.

"I'm so thirsty," the fox said to himself.

"I wish I could have those juicy grapes."

Standing on his back legs, the fox stretched his neck up as far as he could, but the grapes were too high for him to reach.

Then he took several steps backward, ran towards the grapevine, took a giant leap, and … missed!

Determined to get the delicious grapes, the fox ran and jumped, over and over again. Now he was even hotter and thirstier than before, and he still hadn't managed to reach a single grape!

Fed up, the fox stopped jumping. Then he stuck his pointy nose high in the air and trotted away.

"What's all the fuss about grapes, anyway?" he sniffed. "I much prefer strawberries!"

And the moral of the story is: If someone can't get something, they pretend it is not worth having.

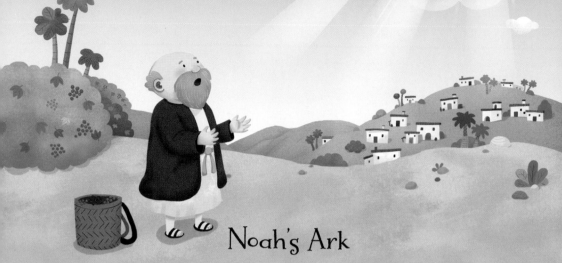

Noah's Ark

Long, long ago, when the world was still new, God looked down and saw that the people on Earth had become wicked. They had forgotten that God wanted them to be good. Instead of helping each other, they spent all their time fighting and hurting one another.

All this wickedness made God unhappy.

But an old man named Noah remembered God. Noah and his family spent their days working hard and being kind to their neighbors and to each other. God was pleased with Noah and his family.

One day, God spoke to Noah.

"The world is too full of wickedness," God said, "and I am going to send a flood to destroy the Earth and everyone on it. But I will keep you and your family safe."

"What must I do?" asked Noah.

"Build a big boat called an ark," said God. "It must be big enough to hold you and your whole family, and two of every animal in the world."

Noah got to work right away. His sons, Ham, Shem, and Japheth, all helped.

They planned and measured … they chopped and sawed … they hammered and heaved … and together, they built a great, strong ark.

At last the ark was ready. Noah's wife, his sons, and his sons' wives all climbed aboard.

Then Noah gathered two of every animal on Earth—every creature that hopped or walked or crawled or flew came to board the ark.

There were cats and bats and rats, monkeys and donkeys, hooting owls and wolves that howled, kangaroos and kinkajous, big baboons and little raccoons—so many animals, of all sorts and shapes and sizes! The ark held them all.

When the last animal had climbed aboard, Noah went inside and shut the door of the ark. Then the rain started to fall.

It rained and rained, and the water rose higher and higher, covering everything on Earth.

Even the tops of the highest mountains were under water!

But the ark floated on the water, and inside, everyone was safe and warm and dry.

Finally, after forty days and forty nights, the rain stopped.

Then strong winds began to blow, drying up the water.

Soon the mountaintops appeared, and the ark came to rest on a mountain called Ararat.

One day Noah sent a raven out of the ark. Soon it came back—it hadn't found anywhere to land.

A week later, Noah sent a dove out.

This time it came back with an olive branch in its beak—so Noah knew that it had found some trees, and that the Earth was almost dry.

Noah waited another week, then sent the dove out again. This time the dove did not come back—it had found a place to land!

"It is time to leave the ark!" Noah told his family. He opened the doors, and all the animals went out—all the birds and beasts, and all the creeping, crawling creatures. They spread out to find homes and raise their families.

Finally, Noah and his family left the ark. They were so happy to be back on dry land!

The first thing Noah did was pray to God to say thank you for keeping him and his family safe from the flood.

Suddenly Noah saw something beautiful in the sky—a bright, shining rainbow!

"This rainbow is a sign of my promise to you, Noah," God said. "I will never again send a flood to destroy the Earth."

These days, whenever we see a rainbow in the sky, we remember Noah, and God's promise to him—and to us.

Claudia's Cauldron

One evening, Claudia was playing in the garden when she found a black pot with three legs.

"That looks just like a magic cauldron," said Claudia. "I wonder if I could cast a spell."

She put some rose petals into the cauldron with some strawberries from the fruit patch and said the magic word, "ABRACADABRA!"

POUF! A large cake decorated with strawberries and sugar roses appeared in front of Claudia.

"Yum!" said Claudia, eating it all up. "What a great cauldron!"

Next, she put into the cauldron a hairbrush, a sugar cube, and a slice of bread. She said the magic word, and POP! A black pony appeared in the garden and started munching the grass.

"Wow," said Claudia in surprise. "I've always wanted a pony!"

She sprang into the saddle and rode around the garden three times. Then she jumped down beside the cauldron once more.

"Now for the biggest spell of all," said Claudia. "A spell to make sure that I never have to go to bed again!"

Into the cauldron she dropped a broken alarm clock, a bedtime story, and a picture of a star. Then she rubbed her hands together in excitement and said the magic word, "ABRACADABRA!"

Claudia waited and waited, but nothing happened.

"I'll try it again," said Claudia, this time calling out the magic word a little louder. "ABRACADABRA!"

But still nothing happened.

"Claudia!" called her daddy from the house. "Time for bed!"

Claudia sighed, and trudged reluctantly toward the house. Even the power of magic couldn't stop bedtime from happening!

The Sorcerer's Apprentice

Once a young boy named Franz worked as an apprentice to a sorcerer.

Every day, the sorcerer gave Franz a long list of chores to do around the castle, while he disappeared into his workshop to chant spells, or journeyed to nearby villages.

But Franz wanted to learn magic! He knew the sorcerer kept a spell book in his workshop, and he longed to read it. So he decided to sneak a look the next time the sorcerer went out.

One day, as the sorcerer was getting ready to leave the castle, he ordered Franz to clean the floor of the Great Hall.

"Fetch the water from the well with this bucket, then carry it to the big stone container in the hall," he said. "When the container is full of water, scrub the floor with this broom."

As soon as the sorcerer left, Franz rushed to get his master's spell book. Inside, Franz saw a spell that could bring objects to life.

"The broom could clean the floor by itself!" he cried, excitedly.

As Franz chanted the spell, the broom suddenly sprouted little arms and leaped into action. It carried the bucket to the well and fetched water to fill the container.

After a while, Franz noticed that the container was overflowing. There was water all over the floor.

"Stop!" he shouted. But the broom didn't stop.

Panicking, Franz grabbed an axe and chopped the broom into small pieces. But the little pieces of broom grew arms too. Soon there was an army of new brooms.

The sorcerer returned just as the overflowing water reached Franz's knees.

"Please forgive me, master," Franz cried. "I just wanted to try magic."

The sorcerer was angry. He chanted a spell, and in an instant the brooms all vanished and the water disappeared.

"You have much to learn," the sorcerer told Franz, sternly.

"I promise to work very hard," the apprentice replied.

"Very well," replied the sorcerer, "you can start by cleaning this floor—the old-fashioned way!"

The Big Race

Lucas the sports car drove along the road next to the railroad track every morning, and he always saw Maisie the train.

"Beep, beep!" he shouted each day. "I'm faster than you!"

"Choo, choo!" Maisie replied. "Oh no, you're not!"

One morning, Maisie said, "I've had enough of that sassy car thinking he's faster than me." So when she saw Lucas, she called out, "I challenge you to a race! First one to the next station is the winner."

"You're on!" chuckled Lucas, swishing his windshield wipers. "But I warn you, I'm sure to win!"

"We'll see about that!" said Maisie with a grin. "Ready, get set, GO!"

Maisie blew her whistle and shot into a tunnel. Lucas screeched around the bend and zoomed under a bridge. What an exciting start to the race!

Maisie was speeding along the track, but then the signal changed, and she had to stop to let another train pass. Lucas whizzed past on the road by the rail tracks.

"See you later, slowcoach!" he hooted.

When the signal changed, Maisie chuffed ahead as fast as she could, puffing and panting. Then she spotted Lucas stuck in a traffic jam on the road ahead.

"Aha!" she said. "I'm catching up after all!"

Lucas weaved through the town, and Maisie rumbled along the track. They were neck and neck! Who would win?

At last Maisie pulled into the station … just as Lucas skidded up outside. It was a draw.

"That was fun!" said Maisie, laughing. "But we still haven't found out who's fastest!"

Just then they heard a loud roar overhead.

"I'm faster than both of you!" shouted Olivia the airplane from high up in the clouds. "Want a race?"

The Frog Prince

Long ago, a princess lived with her father in a palace surrounded by woods.

When it was hot outside, the princess would walk into the shade of the forest and sit by a pond. There she would play with her favorite toy, a golden ball.

One day, the ball slipped from her hand and fell to the bottom of the pond. "My beautiful golden ball," she sobbed.

An ugly, speckled frog popped his head out of the water. "Why are you crying?" he croaked.

"I've dropped my precious golden ball into the water," she cried.

"What will you give me if I get it for you?" asked the frog.

"You may have my jewels," sobbed the unhappy princess.

"I don't need those," said the frog. "If you promise to care for me and be my friend, let me share food from your plate and sleep on your pillow, then I will bring back your golden ball."

"I promise," said the princess, but she thought to herself, "He's only a silly old frog. I won't do any of those things."

When the frog returned with the ball, she snatched it from him and ran back to the palace.

That evening, the princess was having dinner with her father when there was a knock on the door.

When the princess opened the door, she was horrified to find the frog sitting there. She slammed the door and hurried back to the table.

"Who was that?" asked the king.

"Oh, just a frog," replied the princess.

"What does a frog want with you?" asked the puzzled king.

91

The princess told her father about the promise she had made. "Princesses always keep their promises," insisted the king. "Let the frog in and make him welcome."

As soon as the frog hopped through the door, he asked to be lifted up onto the princess's plate. When the frog saw the look of disgust on the princess's face, he sang:

"Princess, princess, fair and sweet, you made a special vow
To be my friend and share your food, so don't forget it now."

The king was annoyed to see his daughter acting so rudely. "This frog helped you," he said. "And now you must keep your promise to him."

For the rest of the day, the frog followed the princess everywhere she went. She hoped that he would go back to his pond when it was time for bed, but when darkness fell, the frog yawned and said, "I am tired. Take me to your room and let me sleep on your pillow."

The princess was horrified. "No, I won't!" she said rudely. "Go back to your pond and leave me alone!"

The patient frog sang:

"Princess, princess, fair and sweet, you made a special vow
To be my friend and share your food, so don't forget it now."

Reluctantly, the princess took the frog to her room. She couldn't bear the thought of sleeping next to him, so she put him on the floor. Then she climbed into her bed and went to sleep.

After a while, the frog jumped up onto the bed. "It's drafty on the floor. Let me sleep on your pillow," he said.

The sleepy princess felt more annoyed than ever. She picked up the frog and hurled him across the room. But when she saw him lying dazed and helpless on the floor, she was suddenly filled with pity.

"Oh, you poor darling!" she cried, and she picked him up and kissed him.

Suddenly, the frog transformed into a handsome young prince.

"Sweet princess," he cried. "I was bewitched, and your tender kiss has broken the curse!"

The prince and princess soon fell in love and were married. They often walked in the shady forest together and sat by the pond, tossing the golden ball back and forth, and smiling at how they first met.

There Was an Old Man from Peru

There was an old man from Peru
Who dreamed he was eating his shoe.
He woke in a fright
In the middle of the night
And found it was perfectly true.

How Many Miles to Babylon?

How many miles to Babylon?
Three score miles and ten.
Can I get there by candlelight?
Yes, and back again.
If your heels are nimble and light,
You may get there by candlelight.

BABYLON

There Was a Little Girl

There was a little girl,
And she had a little curl,
Right in the middle
Of her forehead.

When she was good,
She was very, very good,
But when she was bad,
She was horrid.

As I Was Going to St. Ives

As I was going to St. Ives,
I met a man with seven wives.
Each wife had seven sacks;
Each sack had seven cats;
Each cat had seven kits.
Kits, cats, sacks and wives.
How many were going to St. Ives?

Jack Be Nimble

Jack be nimble,
Jack be quick,
Jack jump over
The candlestick.

Silly Billy

Bats do a lot of things upside down. They eat upside down. They sleep upside down. But Billy Bat spent so much time upside down that he thought up was down!

One night, Billy saw the reflection of the moon in the lake as he hung from his perch.

"I want to fly to the moon," he said.

"Don't be silly, Billy," said his sister, Grace. "The moon is too far away."

"No it's not," said Billy, pointing to the reflection. "It's really close—look!"

Grace shook her head. "You don't understand!" she said.

But Billy wasn't listening.

"Here I go!" he cried. "Wheeee!" He spread his wings and zoomed toward the reflection of the moon in the water. SPLASH! Billy dived into the lake. A few seconds later he crawled out, spluttering, and found his sister waiting for him.

"Do you understand now, Billy?" Grace asked.

"Yes," said Billy, shivering. "The moon is much, much wetter than it looks!"

What a silly Billy!

Fluff's Muddle

Fluff was all in a muddle. During the daytime, when owls should be asleep, Fluff was wide awake. There was just so much happening on the farm! She giggled at the geese waddling around the pond and chuckled as the chickens scratched and pecked the ground. She laughed so much that she kept waking her family up.

"You're too noisy," said her sister, Blink.

"You're keeping us awake!" said her brother, Beak.

That night, Fluff was feeling tired, just when owls should be wide awake.

"I know what we can do to fix Fluff's muddle," said Blink.

Fluff could hardly believe her eyes as Blink and Beak waddled round the pond like geese, and scratched and pecked the ground like chickens. She laughed so much that it kept her awake all night.

By the time morning came, Fluff was feeling very tired indeed. The geese waddled and the chickens scratched and pecked as usual, but Fluff was fast asleep.

The Best Easter Egg Hunt Ever

On a warm spring day, in the tall green grass, a little gray rabbit was sniffing the air.

It was Easter Day. It was egg-hunt time.

Mother Rabbit said, "There are lots of eggs to find. There are stripy eggs and spotty eggs, sky-blue eggs, pale pink eggs, and eggs as bright as buttercups!"

"I want a special egg," said Rabbit. And off she hopped to see what she could find.

Down in the farmyard, Chick was hopping around a haystack.

"Please help me, Rabbit," he cheeped. "I can't reach that egg."

Rabbit hopped onto the haystack in one leap. Nestled in the hay was a sky-blue Easter egg.

"I haven't got much," said Chick. "But I can give you some feathers to say thank you."

Rabbit tucked the feathers into her basket, and off she hopped.

The flowers waved in the breeze, and the air was full of bees. Rabbit hopped with happiness. She followed a fluttering butterfly and nibbled a yellow-green leaf. She picked a bunch of spring flowers.

"Oh," Rabbit laughed. "I almost forgot about finding an egg." And off she hopped …

Rabbit looked for an egg among the tree trunks and in the hedgerows. She found some scraps of sheep's wool stuck in the brambles, but she didn't find a single egg. So off she hopped.

In the sunlit woodland, Rabbit heard a squeak.

"I can't dig up this egg!" said Mouse.

"I'll help," said Rabbit. "I can dig."

SCRAPE. SCRATCH. DIG. BURROW.

"Wow!" breathed Mouse, looking at the giant egg. "It's bigger than our whole mouse hole!" And Mouse gave Rabbit some tasty grass to say thank you.

Rabbit's ears drooped.

"Mouse found a special egg," she sighed. "But I haven't found any."

Rabbit didn't feel like hopping any more. She sat down by the duck pond.

And there, by the water's edge, was an egg. But it wasn't big or bright, spotty or stripy, pink or blue or yellow. It was small and dull and white.

"It doesn't look very special," said Rabbit.

Rabbit touched the egg with her paw. "Oh," she whispered. "It's warm!"

A cold breeze blew. Rabbit shivered.

"Don't worry, little egg," she said. "I'll keep you warm."

And Rabbit emptied out her basket. She took the stalks of grass and the sweet flowers and wove them together. She shaped a little cup. She lined it with warm wool and soft feathers. She made a nest.

And when the egg was safe and warm, Rabbit curled up close by. She was tired after her long day. Soon she was fast asleep.

Peep! Peep!

What was that noise?

Peep! Peep!

It was coming from inside the egg.

The egg wobbled and rocked in the nest, and all the time it went Peep! Peep! PEEP!

Until CRICK! Out came a beak!

And CRACK! Out came …

"A duckling!"

"Quack! Quack!" Mother Duck swam to shore. "Oh, thank you!" she said. "My egg! I've been looking for it all day."

Rabbit smiled. "I'm glad I found this egg," she said. "It's the most wonderful Easter egg of all."

The Big Ship Sails

The big ship sails on the ally-ally-oh,
The ally-ally-oh, the ally-ally-oh.
Oh, the big ship sails on the ally-ally-oh
On the last day of September.

The captain said it will never, never do,
Never, never do, never, never do.
The captain said it will never, never do
On the last day of September.

The big ship sank to the bottom of the sea,
The bottom of the sea, the bottom of the sea.
The big ship sank to the bottom of the sea
On the last day of September.

We all dip our heads in the deep blue sea,
The deep blue sea, the deep blue sea.
We all dip our heads in the deep blue sea
On the last day of September.

If All the World Were Apple Pie

If all the world were apple pie,
And all the sea were ink,
And all the trees were bread and cheese,
What would we have to drink?

A Sailor Went to Sea

A sailor went to sea, sea, sea.
To see what he could see, see, see.
But all that he could see, see, see,
Was the bottom of the deep blue sea, sea, sea.

She Sells Seashells

She sells seashells on the seashore.
The shells she sells are seashells, I'm sure.
For if she sells seashells on the seashore,
Then I'm sure she sells seashore shells.

This rhyme is a tongue twister. Say it as quickly as you can.

The Three Little Pigs

Once upon a time, three little pigs lived together with their mother. One day it was time for them to leave home and build houses of their own.

"Be careful of the big, bad wolf," warned their mother as they trotted off down the road.

The first little pig built his house from straw.

Before long the big, bad wolf came to call.

"Little pig, little pig, let me come in," growled the wolf, licking his lips. He had come for his supper.

"Not by the hairs on my chinny-chin-chin!" the first little pig replied.

"Well, I'll huff and I'll puff and I'll blow your house down!" snarled the wolf. And that's just what he did. The little pig ran away as fast as he could.

The second little pig decided to build his house from sticks.

When the wolf saw the house, he pushed his nose against the door, and growled, "Little pig, little pig, let me come in."

"Not by the hairs on my chinny-chin-chin!" cried the second little pig.

"Well, I'll huff and I'll puff and I'll blow your house down!" snarled the wolf. And that's just what he did. The little pig ran away as fast as he could.

The third little pig built a strong house from bricks. He
had just put a pot of soup on the fire to boil when he saw his
brothers running down the path, closely followed by the wolf.

"Quick!" cried the third little pig. He opened the door and
let his brothers inside.

"Little pigs, little pigs, let me come in!" roared the wolf.

"Not by the hairs on our chinny-chin-chins," cried the
three little pigs.

"Well, I'll huff and I'll puff and I'll blow your house down!"
snarled the wolf. So he huffed and he puffed … and he huffed
and he puffed … but the house stood firm.

The wolf climbed onto the roof and slid down the
chimney—straight into the pot of hot soup.

"Owwwoooo!" he cried.

The wolf leaped up and ran
out of the house, never to
be seen again!

Little Boy Blue

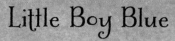

Little Boy Blue,
Come blow your horn.
The sheep's in the meadow,
The cow's in the corn.
Where is the boy who looks after the sheep?
He's under a haystack, fast asleep.
Will you wake him?
No, not I, for if I do, he's sure to cry.

B-I-N-G-O!

There was a farmer had a dog,
And Bingo was his name-o.
B-I-N-G-O
B-I-N-G-O
B-I-N-G-O
And Bingo was his name-o.

Robin and Richard

Robin and Richard were two pretty men,
They lay in bed till the clock struck ten;
Then up starts Robin, and looks at the sky,
"Oh! Oh! Brother Richard, the sun's very high,
You go before with bottle and bag,
And I'll follow after on little Jack Nag."

Gray Goose and Gander

Gray goose and gander,
Waft your wings together,
And carry the good king's daughter
Over the one-strand river.

Old Mother Goose

Old Mother Goose, when
She wanted to wander,
Would ride through the air
On a very fine gander.

Cock-a-Doodle-Doo!

Cock-a-doodle-doo!
My dame has lost her shoe!
My master's lost his fiddling stick,
And doesn't know what to do.

The Old Woman and the Fat Hen

There was once an old woman who kept a hen that laid one egg every morning without fail. The eggs were large and delicious, and the old woman was able to sell them for a very good price at market.

"If my hen would lay two eggs every day," she said to herself, "I would be able to earn twice as much money!"

So, every evening, the old woman fed the hen twice as much food.

Each day the old woman went to the henhouse expecting to find two eggs, but there was still only one—and the hen was getting fatter and fatter.

One morning, the woman looked in the nest box, and there were no eggs at all. There were none the next day, nor any the day after that. All the extra food had made the hen so fat and contented that she had become lazy and had given up laying eggs altogether!

And the moral of the story is: Things don't always work out as planned.

The Mice in Council

Once there was a large family of mice who lived in a big old house. Everything would have been perfect, except for one thing—the cat who lived there too. Each time the mice crept into the kitchen to nibble a few crumbs, the cat would pounce and chase them under the floorboards.

"If we don't come up with a plan soon, we'll starve," cried Grandfather Mouse.

But the mice couldn't agree on a single idea. Finally, the youngest mouse had a brainstorm.

"We could put a bell on the cat's collar so we can hear him coming," he suggested.

All the mice thought this was an excellent plan.

Then Grandfather Mouse stood up. "You are a very smart young fellow to come up with such an idea," he said, "but, tell me—who is going to be brave enough to put the bell on the cat's collar?"

And the moral of the story is: It is sometimes easy to think of a clever plan, but it can be much more difficult to carry it out.

Hansel and Gretel

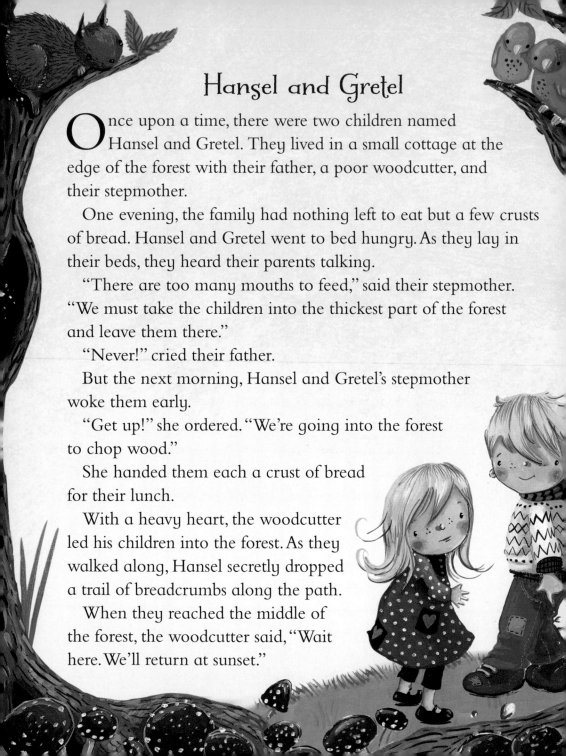

Once upon a time, there were two children named Hansel and Gretel. They lived in a small cottage at the edge of the forest with their father, a poor woodcutter, and their stepmother.

One evening, the family had nothing left to eat but a few crusts of bread. Hansel and Gretel went to bed hungry. As they lay in their beds, they heard their parents talking.

"There are too many mouths to feed," said their stepmother. "We must take the children into the thickest part of the forest and leave them there."

"Never!" cried their father.

But the next morning, Hansel and Gretel's stepmother woke them early.

"Get up!" she ordered. "We're going into the forest to chop wood."

She handed them each a crust of bread for their lunch.

With a heavy heart, the woodcutter led his children into the forest. As they walked along, Hansel secretly dropped a trail of breadcrumbs along the path.

When they reached the middle of the forest, the woodcutter said, "Wait here. We'll return at sunset."

Hansel and Gretel waited all day, but their father and stepmother didn't come back. Soon, it was dark among the thick trees and Gretel was frightened.

"Don't worry," said Hansel, cuddling his sister. "We'll follow the trail of breadcrumbs I dropped along the path. They will lead us home."

But when the moon came up, they couldn't see any crumbs.

"Oh, no! The birds must have eaten them all!" whispered Hansel.

Hansel and Gretel curled up under a tree and fell fast asleep.

The next morning, they wandered through the forest until they came to a little cottage made of gingerbread and cakes!

The children were so hungry they picked cakes off the house and crammed them into their mouths.

Just then, the door opened and an old woman hobbled out.

"Come in, children," she said, smiling. "I've got plenty more food in here."

The old woman fed them well and then put them to bed. But Hansel and Gretel didn't know that the old woman was actually a wicked witch who liked to eat children!

When Hansel and Gretel woke up, the witch grabbed Hansel and locked him in a cage. She set Gretel to work cooking huge meals to fatten up Hansel.

The weeks went by, and every morning the witch went up to the cage, asking Hansel to hold out his finger.

"I want to feel if you are fat enough to eat," she said.

Hansel, being a smart boy, held out an old chicken bone instead. The witch's eyesight was so bad that she thought the bone was Hansel's finger.

One day, the witch got tired of waiting for the boy to get fatter and decided to cook him right away.

Grabbing Gretel's arm, she said, "Go and check if the oven is hot enough." And she pushed Gretel toward the open oven door. Grinning horribly, she licked her cracked lips. She was planning to eat Gretel too, and couldn't wait for her delicious meal.

"I'm too big to fit in there," said Gretel, guessing the witch's wicked plan.

"You silly girl," cackled the witch. "Even I could fit in there." And she stuck her head inside. With a great big shove, Gretel pushed the witch into the oven and slammed the door shut.

"Hansel, the witch is dead!" cried Gretel, unlocking her brother's cage.

As the children made their way out of the house, they found chests crammed with gold and sparkling jewels. They filled their pockets and set off for home.

Their father was overjoyed to see them. He told them that their stepmother had died while they were gone so they had nothing to fear any more. Hansel and Gretel showed their father the treasure.

"We will never go hungry again!" he cried.

And they all lived happily ever after.

I Had Two Pigeons

I had two pigeons, bright and gay,
They flew from me the other day:
What was the reason they did go?
I cannot tell, for I do not know.
Coo-oo, coo-oo!

The Groundhog

If the groundhog sees his shadow,
We will have six more weeks of winter.
If he doesn't see his shadow,
We will have an early spring.

The Little White Duck

There's a little white duck, "Quack!"
Sitting in the water.
A little white duck, "Quack!"
Doing what he oughter.
He took a bite of a lily pad,
Flapped his wings and he said,
"I'm glad I'm a little white duck
Sitting in the water.
Quack, quack, quack!"

The Magpie

Magpie, magpie,
Flutter and flee,
Turn up your tail,
And good luck come to me.

If I Were a Bird

If I were a bird I'd sing a song,
And fly about the whole day long.
And when the night came go to rest,
Up in my cozy little nest.

Haymaking

The maids in the meadow
Are making the hay,
The ducks in the river
Are swimming away.

The Moonlight Tooth Fairy

Twinkle was a tooth fairy. Every night, she flew from house to house collecting the teeth that children had left under their pillows.

Each time she took a tooth, she slipped a shiny coin in its place. Twinkle loved to make people happy, but she often felt lonely.

"I wish I had a friend," she thought.

One night Twinkle came to Isla's house. As she flew through the open window she felt somebody watching her. A fairy face stared at her in the moonlight. And another. There were fairy pictures and toys everywhere!

Twinkle was so surprised she dropped the coin. The noise woke Isla.

Isla gasped when she spotted Twinkle.

Twinkle started to cry. "You've seen me! I've broken the most important fairy rule!"

"Don't cry!" said Isla, gazing at Twinkle in amazement. "I won't tell anyone, I promise."

"And I've lost your coin!" sobbed Twinkle.

Isla had an idea. "Instead of giving me a coin, could you grant me a fairy wish?" she asked.

"What would you wish for?" said Twinkle, drying her tears.

"I wish to be a fairy just like you!"

Twinkle waved magic into the room.

Suddenly Isla felt herself shrinking.

"I'm growing wings!" she cried with joy. "Will you teach me how to fly?"

"It's easy!" said Twinkle. "Hold my hand …"

Twinkle led Isla out into the moonlit garden. They flew between the trees and skimmed a starry pond.

"I love being a fairy!" cried Isla.

"It's much more fun with two," laughed Twinkle happily. At last she had a real friend of her own.

Soon it was time for Isla to go back to being a little girl. "Thank you for making my wish come true," she said to Twinkle.

"You've made my wish come true, too!" replied Twinkle.

Twinkle promised to come back soon.

As she flew away, she whispered, "Sweet dreams, my fairy friend!"

The Naughty Little Rabbits

Once upon a time, three naughty little rabbits lived with their mama in a cozy hillside burrow.

One day, Mama said, "You're getting so big! Come and help me make your sleeping corners bigger."

The naughty little rabbits didn't want to help Mama. "We want to play outside!" they cried.

"First, there is work to do," their mama said. But the naughty little rabbits scampered off to the meadow, leaving their poor mama behind.

"I wish we had someone to play with," said the first little rabbit, looking around for some excitement.

"Why don't you play with me?" cried a squirrel. "Just do what I do and we'll have some fun."

Then the squirrel scampered up a tree and started throwing acorns that rained down upon the naughty little rabbits.

"Ow!" cried the little rabbits, and they ran away.

"I wish we had something to eat," said the second little rabbit, growing hungry after all that running.

"Why don't you have lunch with me?" croaked a little frog. "Just do what I do. Close your eyes and put out your tongues, and you'll catch a yummy fly."

"Yuck! We don't eat flies!" spluttered the little rabbits, pulling their tongues back in and hopping away.

"I wish we could have a cozy nap," said the third little rabbit, tired after so much hopping around.

Before they could curl up, it started to rain. The little rabbits didn't like the rain, and they ran until they reached home.

"We're so sorry, Mama!" cried the little rabbits, as she hugged them close. "Can we help you with the work now?"

"There will be plenty of work for you to do another day," said their mama. "Come and eat your supper, and promise me you won't run off again."

The hungry, sleepy little rabbits ate their supper. Then they crawled into their sleeping corners.

And guess what? Someone had made each one a little bit bigger. Now, who do you think had done that?

Five Little Monkeys

Five little monkeys jumping on the bed,
One fell off and bumped his head.
Mama called the Doctor, and the Doctor said,
"No more monkeys jumping on the bed!"

Four little monkeys jumping on the bed,
One fell off and bumped her head.
Papa called the Doctor, and the Doctor said,
"No more monkeys jumping on the bed!"

*(Repeat the rhyme, counting down from three
little monkeys to one little monkey ...)*

One little monkey jumping on the bed,
He fell off, and bumped his head.
Mama called the Doctor and the Doctor said,
"Put those monkeys straight to bed!"

Three Young Rats

Three young rats with black felt hats,
Three young ducks with white straw flats,
Three young dogs with curling tails,
Three young cats with demi-veils,
Went out for a walk with two young pigs
In satin vests and sorrel wigs.

But suddenly it chanced to rain,
And so they all went home again.

Three Teds in a Tub

Rub-a-dub, dub,
Three teds in a tub,
Sailing across the sea!
But the smell of hot cakes,
And other nice bakes,
Will bring them
Back home for tea.

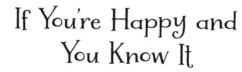

If You're Happy and You Know It

If you're happy and you know it,
Clap your hands.
If you're happy and you know it,
Clap your hands.
If you're happy and you know it,
And you really want to show it,
If you're happy and you know it,
Clap your hands.

If you're happy and you know it,
Nod your head, etc.

If you're happy and you know it,
Stamp your feet, etc.

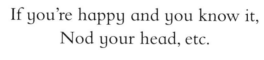

If you're happy and you know it,
Say "We are!," etc.

If you're happy and you know it,
Do all four!

WE ARE!

Teddy Bear, Teddy Bear

Teddy bear, teddy bear,
Touch the ground.
Teddy bear, teddy bear,
Turn around.
Teddy bear, teddy bear,
Walk upstairs.
Teddy bear, teddy bear,
Say your prayers.

Anna Maria

Anna Maria she sat on the fire;
The fire was too hot, she sat on the pot;
The pot was too round, she sat on the ground;
The ground was too flat, she sat on the cat;
The cat ran away with Maria on her back.

Over the Hills and Far Away

When I was young and had no sense
I bought a fiddle for eighteen pence,
And the only tune that I could play
Was "Over the Hills and Far Away."

The Lion and the Mouse

Once upon a time, there was a huge lion who lived in a dark den in the middle of the jungle. If Lion didn't get enough sleep, he became extremely grumpy.

One day, while Lion lay sleeping as usual, a little mouse thought he'd take a short-cut home straight through the lion's den.

"He's snoring so loudly," thought Mouse. "He'll never hear me."

But as he hurried past, he accidentally ran over Lion's paw.

"How dare you wake me up!" Lion roared angrily, grabbing the mouse. "I will eat you for my supper."

"Please," cried Mouse. "I didn't mean to wake you up. I'm too small to make a good meal for someone as mighty as you. Let me go and I promise to help you one day."

Lion laughed loudly. "You're too small to help someone as big as me," he said scornfully, but he opened his paw. "Go home, little mouse."

Mouse looked at Lion in surprise.

"You have made me laugh, so I will let you go," Lion explained. "But hurry, before I change my mind."

"Thank you!" squeaked Mouse gratefully, and he ran home.

A few days later, Lion was hunting in the jungle when he got tangled in a hunter's snare net. He was so angry that he let out the loudest of roars.

"Lion must be in trouble!" squeaked Mouse, and he scurried through the jungle.

"I'll get you out," cried Mouse, when he found the lion, and he started gnawing through the net.

Before long, there was a big hole in the net, and Lion climbed through.

"Thank you," he said humbly. "I was wrong to laugh at you. You saved my life today."

Mouse smiled. "You were kind enough to let me go before," he squeaked. "It was my turn to help you."

And from that day on the huge, mighty lion and the tiny, mighty mouse became the best of friends.

Brown Owl

The brown owl sits in the ivy-bush,
And she looketh wondrous wise,
With a horny beak beneath her cowl,
And a pair of large round eyes.

Butterfly, Butterfly

"Butterfly, butterfly,
Where do you go?"
"Where the sun shines,
And where the buds grow."

Ladybug, Ladybug

Ladybug, ladybug, fly away home;
Your house is on fire, your children all gone,
All except one, and that's little Ann,
And she hid under the baking pan.

Goosey, Goosey, Gander

Goosey, goosey, gander,
Whither do you wander?
Upstairs and downstairs
And in my lady's chamber.
There I met an old man
Who would not say his prayers,
So I took him by the left leg,
And threw him down the stairs.

Dandy

I had a dog and his name was Dandy,
His tail was long and his legs were bandy,
His eyes were brown and his coat was sandy,
The best in the world was my dog Dandy.

I Had a Little Puppy

I had a little puppy,
His name was Tiny Tim.
I put him in the bathtub,
To see if he could swim.
He drank all the water,
He ate a bar of soap—
The next thing I know
He had a bubble in his throat!

127

I Love My Mommy

One morning, Little Deer didn't want to play in his garden any more.

"I want to see new things," he told his mommy.

"Then let's go exploring," said Mommy Deer.

"This way!" cried Little Deer excitedly.

When Little Deer came to the stream, he slowly crossed the wobbly stones, watching the water as it trickled gently beside him.

"Don't get your feet wet," warned Mommy.

"I won't!" said Little Deer, as he wiggled and wobbled.

On the other side of the stream, Little Deer squeezed through the tangly bushes.

"Don't get stuck," warned Mommy.

"I won't! Hurry up, Mommy!" said Little Deer. "Look! A hill that goes up to the clouds!"

Little Deer climbed all the way to the top, panting with each step.

"I can see forever!" cried Little Deer, wobbling as he stood on tiptoes.

Then suddenly …

128

"Wheeee!" cried Little Deer, as he slid down the other side of the hill into a meadow.

"Are you okay?" asked his mommy.

"Yes!" giggled Little Deer. "I am!"

Little Deer looked around the meadow. "Mommy?" he said anxiously. "Which way is home? I'm lost!"

"We'll soon find our way back," Mommy Deer said soothingly. "We just have to remember how we got here."

Little Deer thought and thought. At last, he began to remember …

"We came over the hill!" said Little Deer, and he scampered back up the hill. "I can see the way from here!"

Little Deer and his mommy skidded down the other side of the hill. "We squeezed through those tangly bushes!" cried Little Deer, and they pushed through them.

"Which way now?" said Mommy Deer.

Little Deer heard the tinkling sound of a stream …

"The wobbly stones!" cheered Little Deer. "Don't get your feet wet, Mommy!"

"I won't!" laughed Mommy Deer.

Little Deer knew the way from here. He ran as fast as he could, until he reached his garden.

"I love exploring," cried Little Deer happily. "And I love my mommy!"

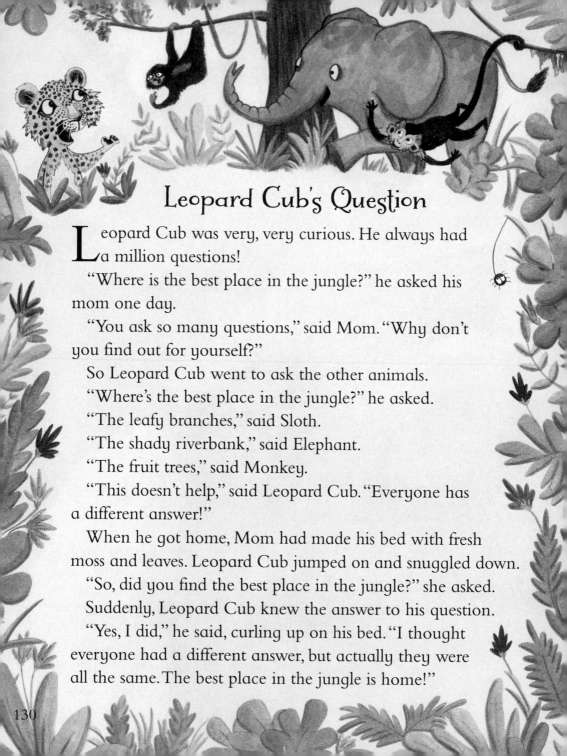

Leopard Cub's Question

Leopard Cub was very, very curious. He always had a million questions!

"Where is the best place in the jungle?" he asked his mom one day.

"You ask so many questions," said Mom. "Why don't you find out for yourself?"

So Leopard Cub went to ask the other animals.

"Where's the best place in the jungle?" he asked.

"The leafy branches," said Sloth.

"The shady riverbank," said Elephant.

"The fruit trees," said Monkey.

"This doesn't help," said Leopard Cub. "Everyone has a different answer!"

When he got home, Mom had made his bed with fresh moss and leaves. Leopard Cub jumped on and snuggled down.

"So, did you find the best place in the jungle?" she asked.

Suddenly, Leopard Cub knew the answer to his question.

"Yes, I did," he said, curling up on his bed. "I thought everyone had a different answer, but actually they were all the same. The best place in the jungle is home!"

Crocodiles Don't Wear Pajamas

There was just one thing that Christopher Crocodile wanted. A pair of pajamas.

"Crocodiles don't wear pajamas," said his father. "We're too tough, and scaly, and scary."

But Christopher had seen a little boy wearing them once, and he had never forgotten.

"Try making some yourself," suggested his mother.

So Christopher gathered large, colorful leaves and star-shaped flowers, and made the most magnificent pair of starry pajamas.

"You look fantastic!" said his mother.

"Fabulous!" said his friends.

All the crocodiles in the swamp started asking for a pair of Christopher's pajamas. He made more … and more … and more!

Nowadays, when the sun is shining, crocodiles look just as tough and scaly and scary as ever. But when the moon comes out and it's time for bed, every single one puts on a wonderful pair of pajamas.

Even Christopher's father!

A Drink for Blaze the Dragon

It was a very hot day, and Blaze's mother was sleeping in the cool cave. But Blaze didn't want to sleep. He wanted to whiz around the mountain. He crept outside.

Wheeee! But flying around in the sizzling heat soon made Blaze thirsty. He flopped down by the lake at the bottom of the valley. Then he remembered his mother's warning:

"Dragons can ONLY drink juniper juice!" she'd told him.

Blaze watched eagerly as a flock of birds drank from the lake. He was too hot to fly all the way home for juniper juice. Surely a little water wouldn't hurt? He licked up a few drops.

"Delicious," Blaze gasped. He dipped his whole face into the lake, and the cold water rushed into his mouth.

Suddenly … PFFFT! Blaze's dragon flames went out.

Blaze was terrified. He flew home as fast as he could.

"Mom," he cried. "I'm not a dragon any more. Look! My fire has gone out!"

"Did you drink the lake water?" asked his mother sternly.

"I did!" he sobbed. "I didn't listen to you."

"There's only one way to get your fire back," she sighed. "We'll have to fly to the volcano. You must swallow its heat."

The burning volcano rumbled and crackled with molten lava as Blaze and his mother flew toward it.

Shaking with fear, the young dragon swooped down as low as he dared and took in a deep, fiery breath.

Blaze landed in the valley below, coughing and spluttering. Suddenly, flickers of orange fire shot out of his nose.

"Mom, it worked—I've got my fire back!" he cried.

Blaze's mother couldn't stay cross with him any more.

"Let's go home," she laughed. "Breathing in that volcano fire must have made you thirsty … for a nice glass of juniper juice!"

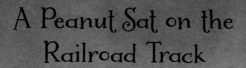

A Peanut Sat on the Railroad Track

A peanut sat on the railroad track,
His heart was all a-flutter;
Along came a train—the 9:15—
Toot, toot, peanut butter!

The Man in the Moon

The man in the moon
Came tumbling down,
And asked his way to Norwich.
He went by the south,
And burned his mouth
By eating cold peas porridge.

Curly Locks

Curly Locks! Curly Locks! Wilt thou be mine?
Thou shalt not wash dishes, nor yet feed the swine,
But sit on a cushion and sew a fine seam,
And feed upon strawberries, sugar, and cream!

Michael Finnegan

There was an old man named Michael Finnegan
He grew whiskers on his chinnegan
The wind came out and blew them in again
Poor old Michael Finnegan. *Begin again …*

Old Betty Blue

Old Betty Blue
Lost a holiday shoe,
What can old Betty do?
Give her another
To match the other,
And then she may swagger in two.

Little Nancy Etticoat

Little Nancy Etticoat, in a white petticoat,
And a red rose.
The longer she stands,
The shorter she grows.

What is she? A candle!

Thumbelina

There was once a poor woman who lived alone in a small cottage. She longed to have a child so, one day, she visited a fairy to ask for her help.

"You are a kind and good woman," said the fairy, "so I will give you this magic seed. Plant it, water it, and you will see what you will see."

The woman thanked the fairy and did as she was told. Soon, a flower bud appeared, with glossy pink petals wrapped tightly around its center.

"What a beautiful flower you will be," smiled the woman. As she bent to kiss the flower, its petals unfolded, and in the center was a beautiful girl, the size of a thumb. The woman was overjoyed.

"I will call you Thumbelina," she cried, and she laid her new child in a walnut-shell bed with a rose-petal quilt.

Thumbelina and her mother were very happy. Then, one day, while her mother was away, an ugly, slimy toad crawled into the cottage and took Thumbelina while she slept.

When she woke up, Thumbelina found herself on a lily pad in the middle of a stream, with two warty toads staring at her.

"This is your new wife!" the mother toad told her warty son.

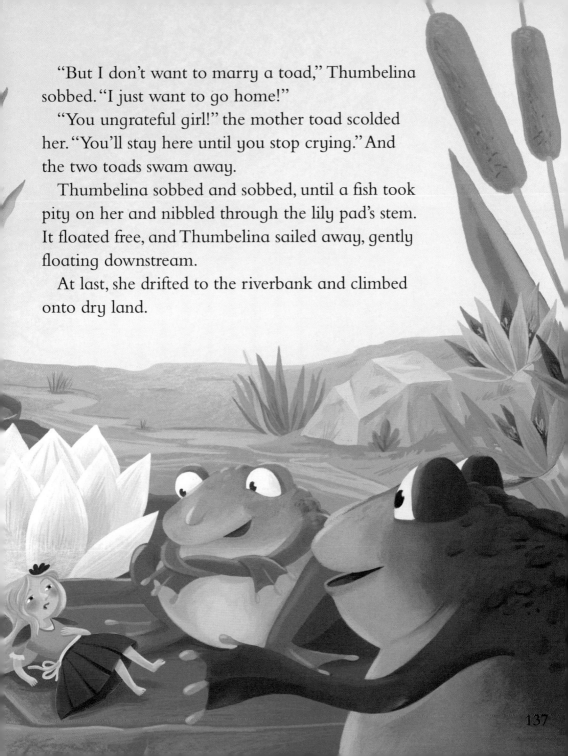

"But I don't want to marry a toad," Thumbelina sobbed. "I just want to go home!"

"You ungrateful girl!" the mother toad scolded her. "You'll stay here until you stop crying." And the two toads swam away.

Thumbelina sobbed and sobbed, until a fish took pity on her and nibbled through the lily pad's stem. It floated free, and Thumbelina sailed away, gently floating downstream.

At last, she drifted to the riverbank and climbed onto dry land.

All that summer, Thumbelina lived in the countryside. She missed her mother terribly, but she busied herself making friends with the birds and small creatures she met.

Then winter came. Thumbelina was cold and hungry. Luckily, a kindly field mouse invited her to stay with him in his burrow. She was so grateful that she said yes at once.

Life underground was warm and snug, but Thumbelina missed the sunshine. And then Mouse's friend Mole asked her to marry him.

"But I don't want to marry a mole," cried Thumbelina.

"You ungrateful girl!" said the mouse. So Thumbelina sadly agreed to marry the mole, and a date was set for the following summer.

Thumbelina was miserable. Then one day, as she walked through the underground tunnels, she found a swallow, almost dead with the cold. She hugged the bird against herself to warm him. He slowly opened his eyes.

"You have saved my life," said the swallow. "Come with me to the south, to the land of sunshine and flowers."

"I cannot leave Mouse," sighed Thumbelina. "He has been so kind to me."

"Then I must go alone," said the swallow. "But I will return next summer. Goodbye!" Then he flew away.

Finally, the day Thumbelina had been dreading arrived—the day she would marry Mole. As she waited for Mole to arrive, the swallow appeared again.

"Come with me now!" he cried.

This time Thumbelina said, "I will!"

So Thumbelina flew away to the south with the swallow, to a land full of flowers. As she bent to smell one especially beautiful flower, the petals opened, and there, in the center, was a fairy prince, no bigger than a thumb, with butterfly wings.

"Will you be my wife?" he asked at once.

"I will!" cried Thumbelina.

So Thumbelina married the fairy prince and became queen of the flower fairies. She did not forget her dear mother, and arranged for fairy messengers to deliver a letter to her with a bouquet of beautiful flowers.

Thumbelina and her handsome prince lived happily ever after.

Pansy Pig

Mrs. Pig had five beautiful piglets. But from the moment they were born, they were TROUBLE!

There was Percy, who loved to stick his little pink snout into everything; Pickle, who was always getting lost; Poppy and Pippa, who tried to eat the strangest things; and Pansy … She wasn't that naughty, but somehow, she got into more trouble than all the other four piglets put together!

The thing is, Pansy's brothers and sisters all looked so alike. They were pink all over, and Mrs. Pig found it very hard to tell them apart.

But Pansy was different. She was pink with a brown pansy-shaped mark on her bottom. So whenever the piglets were up to no good, Mrs. Pig could always spot Pansy.

"No, Pansy! Stop being so naughty," Mrs. Pig would yell. Poor Pansy! Her brown patch gave her away every time.

"It's not fair," she snorted. "I always get the blame just because Mommy can tell me apart."

Then, one rainy day, the five little piglets were playing on the muddy bank by the pond … They skidded and slipped, they splished and sploshed, and soon, they were covered with mud from their ears to their trotters.

When Mrs. Pig found the messy piglets, she wasn't happy.

"Pansy!" she shouted without thinking … But Pansy's familiar little marking on her bottom was nowhere to be seen.

Mrs. Pig started to giggle. Then she burst out laughing. And she jumped into the mud with a big SPLAT!

"I love getting muddy!" squealed Pansy Pig.

"Me too," chortled Mrs. Pig. "Oh, Pansy, is that you? You look just like your brothers and sisters today."

And for once, Pansy didn't get the blame. She was just a muddy little piglet like the others.

Bunnies All Come Out to Play

Bunnies all come out to play,
In the sunshine of the day.
They bounce and run and hop around,
Until they hear a scary sound!
At first they freeze—then off they bound,
And dart away beneath the ground.

The Seesaw

You go up and I go down,
But then we switch it all around.
Now you go down and I go high,
High enough to touch the sky!

This Little Piggy

This little piggy went to market,
This little piggy stayed home,
This little piggy had roast beef,
This little piggy had none,
And this little piggy cried,
"Wee, wee, wee!" all the way home.

Dickery Dare

Dickery, dickery, dare,
The pig flew up in the air.
The man in brown
Soon brought him down!
Dickery, dickery, dare.

To Market, to Market

To market, to market, to buy a fat pig,
Home again, home again, jiggety-jig.
To market, to market, to buy a fat hog,
Home again, home again, jiggety-jog.
To market, to market, to buy a plum cake,
Home again, home again, market is late.
To market, to market, to buy a plum bun,
Home again, home again, market is done.

The Golden Goose

There was once a poor boy named Billy, who lived with his family at the edge of a forest. One day when he was cutting wood, an old man approached him.

"Could I please share some of your food?" the man asked.

"Of course," said Billy, although he barely had enough food for himself.

"Thank you," said the old man. "You shall be rewarded. Cut down that tree over there and see what's inside it."

So he did. Hidden inside the tree trunk was a goose with golden feathers! Puzzled, Billy looked around for the old man, but he had mysteriously vanished.

It was getting too dark to walk home, so Billy picked up the goose and took it with him to an inn.

The innkeeper's three daughters were fascinated by the goose's golden feathers. But when the eldest girl tried to take one, she stuck fast to the goose. As her sisters tried to pull her away, they all got stuck to each other.

The next morning, Billy set off down the street with the golden goose, dragging the girls behind him.

When other people saw the strange scene, they tried to pull the girls free, only to become stuck too!

Meanwhile, the king had a daughter who never laughed. The king was so desperate to cheer her up that he had promised her hand in marriage to anyone who could make her happy.

When the princess looked out of her palace window that day, she saw Billy walking along the street carrying a golden goose with a line of people staggering behind. The princess laughed and laughed.

The king was delighted. "You made the princess laugh!" he told Billy. "That means you may marry her!"

"Me?" Billy cried, just as the goose jumped from his arms. All the people toppled backward, unstuck, and the princess laughed again.

So Billy and the princess soon married, and they lived long, happy lives full of laughter.

The Queen of Hearts

The Queen of Hearts, she made some tarts
All on a summer's day.
The Knave of Hearts, he stole the tarts
And took them all away.
The King of Hearts called for the tarts
And beat the Knave full sore.
The Knave of Hearts brought back the tarts
And vowed he'd steal no more.

Simple Simon

Simple Simon met a pieman,
Going to the fair;
Said Simple Simon to the pieman,
"Let me taste your ware."
Said the pieman to Simple Simon,
"Show me first your penny."
Said Simple Simon to the pieman,
"Indeed, I have not any!"

Jelly on the Plate

Jelly on the plate,
Jelly on the plate,
Wibble, wobble,
Wibble, wobble,
Jelly on the plate.

Bunny Loves to Learn

One morning, Buster Bunny and his best friends Sam the squirrel, Max the mouse, and Francine the frog arrived at school.

"What's in those boxes, Miss?" asked Buster.

"Costumes!" said Miss Nibbler. "Today you're going to dress up as people who lived a long time ago. I want you to make something from the time when they lived, and tell us all about it!"

"I'm going to find out about Vikings," said Buster.

"I want to be a knight," said Sam. "They have amazing helmets!"

"I think I'll be a princess!" cried Francine.

"I can't decide what to find out about," said Max.

"Why don't you dress up as an Egyptian ruler?" said Buster, taking a book from the shelf. "They were called pharaohs."

But the pharaoh's crown was missing from the box.

"I don't want to be a king without a crown!" said Max.

Just then he noticed a poster on the classroom wall.

"I want to be an Egyptian mummy!" he said. "They're so cool!"

148

He rummaged in the costume box.

"Bother," he said. "There's no mummy costume."

"I've got a knight's sword and helmet," said Sam. "I'm going to make a shield to go with them."

"I'm building a model of a Viking ship," said Buster.

"And I'm making a palace for a princess," said Francine.

Soon Buster, Sam, and Francine were busy making things. But Max still didn't know what to make.

"I really want to dress as a mummy," he grumbled.

"What else do you know about Egyptians?" asked Buster.

"I know they built big pyramids," said Max.

"Why don't you build one of those?" suggested Buster.

Max found some big sheets of cardboard and tried to make a pyramid.

"Oh dear," he said. "This is trickier than I thought."

Francine showed him how to look up pyramids on the computer.

"Ah, now I see," said Max. "A pyramid has four sides, not three. And each side is exactly the same size."

Max finished his pyramid proudly, but then he sighed. "I still don't know what to wear!" he said.

"Ouch!" said Buster suddenly. "I just got a paper cut!"

"It's only a small one," said Miss Nibbler. "But you'd better go to the school nurse for a bandage."

"That gives me an idea!" said Buster. He whispered in Max's ear.

"Great!" laughed Max. "Please don't be long!"

When it was time to present to the class, the friends took turns showing what they had made.

"I'm a knight," said Sam. "My shield protected me in battle. It was brightly painted so that my friends could recognize me when my helmet was shut!"

"I'm a princess," said Francine. "I lived in a palace. I wore long silky dresses and tall pointy hats. And I often got to boss around all the knights!"

Buster, back from the nurse, showed the class his Viking ship. "I'm a Viking," he said. "I loved to sail in a very fast ship called a longship. It had a dragon's head carved on the front to scare my enemies!"

"Thanks, Buster," said Miss Nibbler. "Now it's Max's turn."

"Egyptians lived a very, very long time ago," said Max's voice. But he was nowhere to be seen …

"They built amazing pyramids," the voice went on. "The pyramids were taller than ten houses on top of each other! Nobody lived in them, except for—MUMMIES! RAAAAH!"

And Max leaped out of the pyramid.

"So that's where you were hiding!" cried Francine.

"Where did you get that wonderful mummy costume?" asked Sam. "I thought there wasn't one."

"I borrowed the bandages from the school nurse," said Max. "It was Buster's idea."

"Clever thinking, Buster!" said Miss Nibbler. "And well done to everybody. Your costumes look amazing, and you've all learned some really interesting things. What a wonderful show and tell!"

Elephants Never Forget

I woke up this morning, astounded,
To find my long trunk in a knot!
I know it must be to remind me
To remember something I forgot!

But though I've been thinking all morning
I haven't remembered it yet.
Still I'm sure I will think of it soon,
Because elephants never forget!

A Nutty Adventure

Squirrel was scurrying around the forest floor, gathering nuts for winter. Then, when he was sure nobody was looking, he pushed them, one by one, into his secret hidey-hole at the bottom of the Giant Beech.

It was hard work, and soon Squirrel needed a break. He peeped into the hole to see how many nuts he had collected.

But the hidey-hole was empty!

Squirrel was so angry that he stamped his feet and squeaked at the top of his voice, "Someone's stolen my pile of nuts!"

Rabbit hopped over to her friend, rubbing her head.

"Well, someone has been dropping nuts on me," she cried. "I've just had to sweep them all out of my house."

Then Rabbit began to laugh. She realized what had happened. Squirrel had been pushing the nuts through her window!

When Rabbit explained, Squirrel began to chuckle too.

"What a nutty adventure!" he laughed.

The Three Billy Goats Gruff

Long ago, there were three brothers—a little goat, a medium-sized goat, and a big goat.

The brothers lived in a field of short, dry grass beside a river.

On the other side of the river, over a bridge, was a huge meadow with long, juicy grass.

The goats longed to taste the juicy grass, but the bridge was guarded by a horrible, ugly troll.

One day, the little Billy Goat Gruff plucked up his courage and trotted over the bridge.

TRIP TRAP, TRIP TRAP went his feet.

"Who's that TRIP TRAPPING over my bridge?" cried the troll, leaping in front of the little goat. "I will eat you!"

"Please don't!" cried the little goat.

"Wait for my brother—he is much bigger and tastier than me."

"All right," said the greedy troll, and he let the little goat cross.

Later that day, the medium-sized goat saw his little brother munching juicy grass on the other side, and wanted to eat it, too.

So he set off, TRIP TRAP, TRIP TRAP, across the bridge.

"Who's that TRIP TRAPPING over my bridge?" cried the troll again. "I will eat you!"

"Please don't!" cried the medium-sized goat. "Wait for my brother—he is much bigger and tastier than me."

The greedy troll licked his lips, and let the medium-sized Billy Goat Gruff cross the bridge.

At last it was the big Billy Goat Gruff's turn to cross the bridge. TRIP TRAP, TRIP TRAP went his hooves on the wooden bridge.

"Who's that TRIP TRAPPING over my bridge?" bellowed the troll, drooling at the sight of the big goat. "I will eat you!"

But the big Billy Goat Gruff was not afraid of the ugly troll.

"You can't eat me!" shouted the big Billy Goat Gruff. He lowered his head, stamped his hooves, and tossed the troll into the river with his great big billy goat horns.

Then the biggest goat went TRIP TRAP, TRIP TRAP over the bridge to join his brothers, and the horrible troll never bothered them again!

Dance, Jiggle, Dance

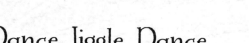

The animals at Red Barn Farm were fed up. They wanted some peace and quiet, but Jiggle, the donkey, was tap dancing. He was practicing for the local farm dance competition. His hooves clicked and clattered loudly across the yard as he twirled, and his shrill braying could be heard for miles around as he sang along. He was determined to win. But first, he had to find a dance partner.

Jiggle clattered over to the pond to ask Duck.

"I'd like to help," quacked Duck, "but I've got flat feet."

Jiggle clopped over to the barn to ask Cow.

"I can't," mooed Cow. "If I dance around my milk gets too frothy. Why don't you ask Sheep?"

"Will you dance with me?" Jiggle asked Sheep.

"Oh, I've got such a thick coat," bleated Sheep. "I'll get too hot."

Jiggle wouldn't give up! Even though he didn't have a partner, he practiced his dance moves all week.

At last, the day of the competition arrived. All the competitors gathered in the big tent, set up on the village green. Jiggle still hadn't found a dance partner, but he decided to watch Farmer Brown and Mrs. Brown, who were dancing first. Everyone cheered as they made their way to the stage, but suddenly, Farmer Brown tripped and hurt his knee.

"I'm fine," he told Mrs. Brown, "just go ahead without me."

Mrs. Brown looked around and saw Jiggle.

"Will you be my partner?" she asked. "The other animals have told me all about your dancing."

Beaming with pride, Jiggle joined Mrs. Brown on the dance floor. What a pair they made, moving together in perfect rhythm!

When the judge announced that they had won first prize, it was the happiest day of Jiggle's life.

Now, the other animals don't mind Jiggle's dancing quite so much. They even stop what they are doing to watch his new moves! However, if Jiggle breaks into song as he dances, the other animals just cover their ears and yell, "Please, Jiggle, just jiggle."

The Ugly Duckling

Once there was a proud and happy duck. "I have seven beautiful eggs, and soon I will have seven beautiful ducklings," she told her friends on the riverbank.

A while later she heard a CRACK! One beautiful duckling popped her little head out of a shell. And then another … and another … until there were six beautiful little ducklings, drying their fluffy yellow wings in the spring air.

"Just one egg left," quacked Mother Duck, "and it's a big one!"

For a while, nothing happened. Then, at last, the big egg began to hatch.

Tap, tap, tap! Out came a beak.

Crack, crack, crack! Out popped a head.

Crunch, crunch, crunch! Out came the last duckling.

"Oh, my!" gasped Mother Duck, "Isn't he … different?"

The last little duckling did look strange. He was bigger than the other ducklings and he didn't have such lovely yellow feathers.

"That's okay," said Mother Duck. "You may look different but you're special to me."

When Mother Duck took her little ducklings for a swim, each one landed in the river with a little plop. But the ugly duckling fell over his big feet and landed in the water with a big SPLASH! The other ducklings laughed at their clumsy brother.

"Hush now, little chicks," said Mother Duck. "Stick together and stay behind me!"

Back at the nest, the ducklings practiced their quacking.

"Quack, quack, quackety-quack!" said the ducklings, repeating after Mother Duck.

"Honk! Honk!" called the ugly duckling.

The other ducklings all quacked with laughter.

The ugly duckling hung his head in shame.

"I'll never fit in," he thought sadly.

The next day, Mother Duck took her little ones out for another swim. The little ducklings stayed close to her while the ugly duckling swam alone.

"What kind of a bird are you?" asked some geese, who had landed on the river nearby.

"I'm a duckling," he replied. "My family has left me all alone."

The geese felt sorry for the ugly duckling, and asked him to go with them. But the ugly duckling was too afraid to leave his river, so he stayed put.

When Mother Duck wasn't looking, the other ducklings teased their ugly brother.

"Look at his dull, gray feathers," said one of his sisters unkindly, admiring her own reflection in the water. "Mine are so much prettier."

The ugly duckling swam away and looked at his reflection.

"I don't look the same as them," he thought, sadly.

So he swam down the river and didn't stop until he'd reached a place he had never seen before. "I'll stay here," he decided.

Summer turned to fall. The sky became cloudy and the river murky. But still the ugly duckling swam alone in his quiet part of the river.

Snow fell heavily that winter, and the ugly duckling was cold and lonely. The river was frozen solid.

"At least I can't see my ugly reflection any more," he thought.

Spring arrived at last, and the ice thawed.

Some magnificent white ducks arrived on the river, and swam toward the ugly duckling.

"You're very big ducks," he said, nervously.

"We're not ducks," laughed the elegant creatures. "We're swans—just like you!"

Puzzled, the ugly duckling looked at his reflection in the river and was surprised to see beautiful white feathers and an elegant long neck.

"Is that really me?" he asked.

"Of course," they told him. "You are a truly handsome swan!"

The handsome young swan joined his new friends and glided gracefully back up the river with them.

When he swam past a family of ducks, Mother Duck recognized her ugly duckling right away. "I always knew he was special," she said.

And the beautiful young swan swam down the river proudly, ruffling his spectacular white feathers and holding his elegant head high.

I Won't Budge!

The animals were hot and bothered. There had been no rain for days, and the watering hole was beginning to dry up under the hot African sun.

"Let's take turns cooling down in the water," suggested the antelope, and all the other animals agreed.

But when the hippo took his turn, he refused to come out of the water.

"You're not being fair," shouted the other animals. "We all want a chance."

"No way," said the hippo. "It's far too nice in here … I WON'T BUDGE!"

"That's so mean," cried the animals. "Please let us have a turn."

But the selfish hippo just chanted, "I WON'T BUDGE! I WON'T BUDGE!"

As the sun grew hotter, more animals came to the watering hole. Still the hippo wouldn't budge.

Suddenly, a thundering noise boomed across the plains, followed by a huge thirsty elephant heading right for the watering hole!

All the animals fled, including the hippo, as the elephant charged into the water. SPLASH!

Once the elephant was settled,
the other animals returned.

"Now the elephant won't budge,"
the hippo grunted.

"Well, you did the same to us,"
huffed the antelope.

The elephant heard this conversation
and felt sorry for the sweltering animals.
So he had an idea …

"One … two … three … SQUIRT!" trumpeted
the elephant.

"Aaaaah!" sighed the animals, as the spray cooled
them down.

But the hippo had been left out.

"Hey, can I have some?" he asked.

"No," said the elephant. "Now you know how it feels."

The hippo drooped his head in shame and
turned away.

After a few minutes, the huge elephant shouted,
"I think you've learned your lesson."

He grinned at the other animals and cried,
"One … two … three … SQUIRT!"

"Thank you!" sighed the hippo, as the
cool water splashed against his hot skin.
"I won't budge from HERE now!"

Two Little Dickie Birds

Two little dickie birds sitting on a wall,
One named Peter, one named Paul.
Fly away Peter, fly away Paul.
Come back Peter, come back Paul.

Ten Green Bottles

Ten green bottles standing on the wall,
Ten green bottles standing on the wall,
And if one green bottle should accidentally fall,
There'd be nine green bottles standing on the wall.

You can keep counting down until there are no more bottles!

Magic Seed

I found a tiny little seed and planted it outside.
Almost at once it started to grow up, tall and wide.
It sprouted leaves from everywhere, and soon became quite big.
I'm not sure what it is yet—apples, pears, or figs?
No matter how it turns out, I know that it will be
My own completely special something-or-other tree!

Song of the Sky Loom

O our Mother the Earth, O our Father the sky,
Your children are we, and with tired backs
We bring you the gifts that you love.
Then weave for us a garment of brightness;
May the warp be the white light of morning,
May the weft be the red light of evening,
May the fringes be the falling rain,
May the border be the standing rainbow.
Thus weave for us a garment of brightness,
That we may walk fittingly where birds sing,
That we may walk fittingly where grass is green,
O our Mother the Earth, O our Father the sky.

Tweedledum and Tweedledee

Tweedledum and Tweedledee
Agreed to have a battle,
For Tweedledum said Tweedledee
Had spoiled his nice new rattle.
Just then flew down a monstrous crow,
As black as a tar-barrel,
Which frightened both the heroes so,
They quite forgot their quarrel.

Dillon the Digger's Challenge

It was Dillon the digger's first day on the building site, and he was nervous. He had to dig twenty holes for posts to go in. It was the biggest job Dillon had ever done, and the other machines didn't seem very friendly at first.

"You're very little," grumbled the cement mixer.

"I hope you're a fast worker," said the crane.

"I'll try my best," Dillon whispered.

Dillon dug and scooped and shoveled. Faster and faster! Then the crane lifted the posts into place, and the mixer poured in the concrete. At last the job was finished, right at the end of the day.

"You might be small, but you're speedy," said the crane, as they settled down for the night.

"Welcome to the team!" added the mixer.

Dillon felt tired but proud. It was good to be needed, and he couldn't wait for another busy day of digging!

The Best Builder

Max was the best builder in the world. He could build anything. He built tall skyscrapers and huge castles and long bridges. Max was so good he became the boss and told everyone what to do instead of hammering and sawing himself. But one day on site, he realized that he was bored.

"Watching other people building is no fun," he said.

There was a meadow with trees in it behind the building site. Max peeped over the wall and saw a boy and his mother building a tree house.

"Can I help?" asked Max.

Max, the boy, and his mother worked all day. They built walls and windows and a long, long ladder.

"This is the best tree house EVER!" said the boy.

Max decided to quit being the boss.

"I love hammering and sawing, not telling people what to do!" he said.

Nowadays, Max won't work on big buildings. He builds tree houses instead!

The Nutcracker

It was Christmas Eve, and Clara and her brother Fritz were very excited. That night there was going to be a magnificent party at their house.

Fritz was busy playing with his toy soldiers, while Clara finished decorating their enormous tree with a beautiful fairy in a sugarplum-colored dress.

At last, the guests started arriving for the party.

"Look, there's Godfather Drosselmeyer!" said Fritz.

Their godfather was a famous toymaker. He hugged the children close, and then gave them their gifts.

Fritz eagerly unwrapped a mechanical jawbreaker machine. For Clara, there was a wooden nutcracker in the shape of a soldier.

"I love him," Clara whispered. "Thank you, Godfather."

"But he's a soldier," said Fritz. "He should be mine."

Fritz tried to snatch the Nutcracker away from her. He pulled and Clara tugged, and then … CRACK!

The Nutcracker's leg snapped off!

"I can fix him, Clara," said their godfather gently. He pulled a little tool pouch from his pocket and quickly mended the Nutcracker.

"Oh, thank you," cried Clara. She placed the Nutcracker carefully under the Christmas tree and went to join the party.

Finally, the last dance was danced and the guests said their
goodbyes. The family went to bed, and the house was dark
and quiet.

BONG! BONG!

Clara awoke to hear the clock striking midnight. She
suddenly remembered she'd left the Nutcracker under the tree,
so she tiptoed downstairs. As she bent down to pick him up,
the tree suddenly started to grow! Or was it that Clara
was shrinking?

"What's happening?" she cried.

"Don't be afraid," said a kind voice.

Clara turned around. Her Nutcracker had come alive!
Behind him, Fritz's soldiers were sitting up in their toybox.

Before Clara could speak, she heard a scurrying sound, and
an army of mice poured into the room, led by a giant Mouse
King with a golden crown.

"Attack!" he squeaked.

"To battle!" ordered the Nutcracker, and Fritz's soldiers
marched boldly toward the attacking mice.

Suddenly, Clara saw the Mouse King spring at the Nutcracker. She snatched off her slipper and hurled it at the Mouse King. He fell to the ground, and his crown tumbled from his head.

With their leader defeated, the mice scurried away in fear.

The Nutcracker picked up Clara's slipper. "I owe you my life, Clara," he said. "You broke the spell that was put on me long ago by a wicked Mouse Queen."

Clara gasped—the Nutcracker had been transformed into a handsome prince!

"Come," said the prince, as he helped Clara into a magical sleigh. "I'll take you on a wonderful adventure."

The walls of the sitting room seemed to fade away, and a sleigh drew up. They climbed aboard, and it flew high into the starry sky.

"Where are we?" gasped Clara.

"This is the Kingdom of Sweets," said the prince.

Gently, the sleigh landed beside a magnificent marzipan palace.

"Look," said the prince, waving to a fairy by the gate. "It's the Sugarplum Fairy!"

"Prince Nutcracker!" cried the fairy. "You are home at last!"

"This is Princess Clara," said the prince. "She saved my life and broke the Mouse Queen's spell."

The Sugarplum Fairy hugged Clara. "Let's celebrate!" she said.

Inside the palace, Clara and the prince feasted on delicious cakes and sweets. They watched in wonder as the Sugarplum Fairy twirled around the room to the beautiful music.

Clara's eyelids began to droop and the sound of the music became fainter and fainter …

When Clara woke up on Christmas morning, she found herself curled up under the Christmas tree next to the Nutcracker.

"I've had the most wonderful adventure," sighed Clara, and she told her parents all about it.

"It was just a dream, darling," said her mother.

Clara gazed up at the sugarplum-colored fairy on top of the tree. Then she looked at the wooden Nutcracker in her hands.

"Perhaps it was," she said. But then, Clara noticed something glinting on the carpet, and a smile spread across her face.

It was a tiny golden crown.

Humpty Dumpty

Humpty Dumpty sat on a wall,
Humpty Dumpty had a great fall.
All the king's horses, and all the king's men
Couldn't put Humpty together again!

Three Blind Mice

Three blind mice, three blind mice,
See how they run, see how they run!
They all ran after the farmer's wife,
Who cut off their tails with a carving knife.
Did you ever see such a sight in your life
As three blind mice?

See a Pin

See a pin and pick it up,
All the day you'll have good luck;
See a pin and let it lay,
Bad luck you'll have all the day!

I Eat My Peas with Honey

I eat my peas with honey,
I've done it all my life,
It makes the peas taste funny,
But it keeps them on my knife.

Little Miss Muffet

Little Miss Muffet
Sat on a tuffet,
Eating her curds and whey.
Along came a spider,
Who sat down beside her
And frightened Miss Muffet away!

173

Tractor Mayhem

It was a beautiful sunny day on Friendship Farm, but Hank Hayseed couldn't enjoy it just yet. He had work to do.

"When you're finished we can have a picnic down by the duck pond," said his wife, Molly. "I'll just pop into town for some groceries."

Hank and his sheepdog Gus watched Molly drive off in her old jeep.

"We'll get the chores done in no time if we use my tractor," said Hank.

Gus wasn't so sure. That tractor was pretty old! And sure enough, the moment Hank started the engine, black smoke came pouring out.

"Oh, rats!" said Hank. "What am I going to do now?"

Then he had a crackerjack idea. Hank pushed the tractor into his workshop, closed the doors and set to work. The farm animals gathered round, trying to peek in and see what he was doing.

"Every time he tries to fix something, he only makes it worse," clucked Mrs. Beak.

"Here he comes," said Gus. "Let's skedaddle!"

Hank rode out on his tractor. "Yee-harr!" he hollered, waving his hat like a cowboy at a rodeo.

The old tractor looked as good as new. Hank had fixed it up, given it a lick of paint—and fitted rocket boosters!

"With a vehicle like this, we'll be the best farm in the whole county!" Hank said proudly. "Hop aboard, Gus—we've got work to do!"

Hank pulled the lever. Flames shot out of the rocket boosters, and the tractor zoomed off!

Bailey the horse saw the tractor roaring toward him carrying hay for his breakfast.

"About time," he neighed. "I'm starving."

Hank pulled the lever to stop the tractor—and that's when everything started to go wrong. Instead of stopping, the tractor went faster! As it shot past, a hay bale flew off the trailer and landed—THUNK!—on Bailey's head.

"Sorry, Bailey!" Hank called back over his shoulder.

Hank wrestled with the pesky lever. But it was no use…and now they were heading for old Maggie the cow.

"The lever's stuck fast!" Hank cried as Gus held on.

"I do believe," said Maggie grandly, "it is rude for anyone to move that fast."

But she moved fast enough herself when she saw the tractor was coming straight for her … and wasn't going to stop!

Up ahead, Mrs. Beak and her ducklings were paddling on the pond. As the tractor splashed through the water, a wave sent them flying!

"We've got to stop this thing!" said Hank, grappling with the lever. He gave an almighty tug—and it came off in his hands.

"Jumping jelly beans!" Hank cried. "We're out of control!"

And that's when Molly arrived home.

"Are you okay?" she cried.

"Yes, dear!" Hank called back. "Just taking Wallow a bucket of pig food!"

Hank held up the bucket to show Molly as the tractor whizzed past her. Then they hit a bump and the bucket went flying out of his hands ... and landed on Molly's head!

"Hold on tiiiiiiight!" yelled Hank as the tractor zoomed up the sloping roof of Wallow the pig's sty as if it were a ramp. It shot into the air ... and landed slap-bang in the middle of the duck pond!

Hank and Gus were soaked, and Friendship Farm was a terrible mess.

"This'll take all day to fix!" groaned Hank.

"Nonsense!" said Molly, still pulling food scraps from her hair. "We can do it and still have time for a picnic, just as long as we all pitch in and work together!"

And everyone agreed that was a crackerjack idea.

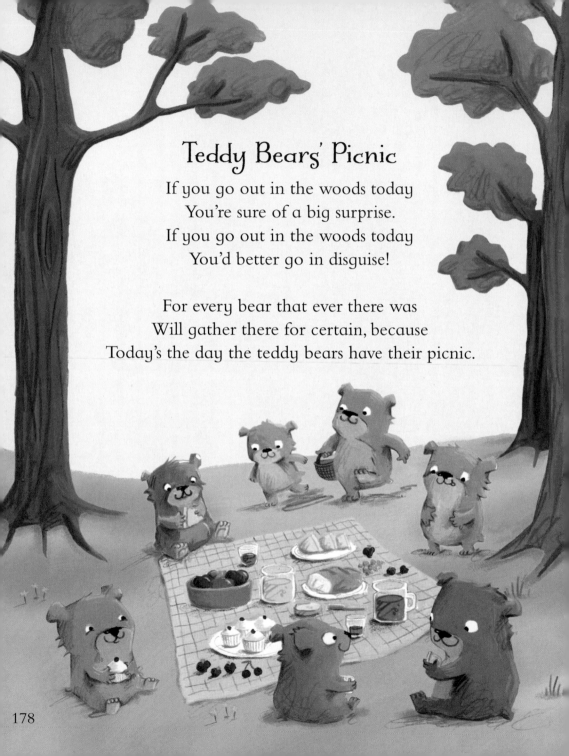

Teddy Bears' Picnic

If you go out in the woods today
You're sure of a big surprise.
If you go out in the woods today
You'd better go in disguise!

For every bear that ever there was
Will gather there for certain, because
Today's the day the teddy bears have their picnic.

Peter Piper

Peter Piper picked a peck of pickled peppers;
A peck of pickled peppers Peter Piper picked;
If Peter Piper picked a peck of pickled peppers,
Where's the peck of pickled peppers Peter Piper picked?

This rhyme is a tongue-twister. Say it as quickly as you can.

The Man from the Moon

Most people think that the moon is empty. It certainly looks empty. But there's a man who lives there who is very clever, and he knows how to hide.

Every night, the man from the moon puts on his space suit, steps into his candy-striped rocket, and zooms off into space to explore the planets. But you never see him because he always takes off from the other side of the moon.

"I love space!" said the man from the moon one night, as he shot past stars and planets. "Get ready for an adventure, little rocket. Tonight, we're going to visit a new world!"

They landed on a very strange planet. It was covered with forests of bendy trees.

The man from the moon climbed the trees and played with some purple aliens who lived in them. He swung from the branches by his toes and waved to everyone he saw.

"This is the best planet ever!" he said. "I wish there was somewhere like this on the moon!"

The purple aliens were very curious about the rocket. They climbed on it and peered into it and patted it. And while the man from the moon was looking the other way, the bravest alien of all crept inside and hid under the seat.

When it was time to leave, the aliens gave the man from the moon some snacks for his journey. He waved goodbye and blasted off in his candy-striped rocket. But halfway home, the stowaway alien crawled out from under his seat! A big, beaming smile spread across the face of the man from the moon.

"There's going to be a little bit of the forest on the moon after all!" he cheered.

Most people think that the moon is empty. But the man who lives there is very clever at hiding himself … and so is his new alien friend!

Sleeping Beauty

Once upon a time, a king and queen had a beautiful baby girl. The proud parents decided to hold a christening feast to celebrate, so they invited kings, queens, princes and princesses from other kingdoms.

Five good fairies lived in the kingdom, and the king wanted them to be godmothers to his daughter. One of these fairies was very old, and no one had seen her in years or even knew where she was. So when the king sent out the invitations, he invited only the four young fairies.

The day of the christening arrived, and the palace was full of laughter and dancing.

After the delicious feast, the four fairies gave the princess their magical gifts.

The first fairy waved her wand over the crib and said, "You shall be kind and considerate."

The second fairy said, "You shall be beautiful and loving."

The third fairy said, "You shall be clever and thoughtful …"

Suddenly the palace doors flew open. It was the old fairy. She was furious because she hadn't been invited to the feast.

She flew up to the crib and waved her wand over the princess.

"One day the king's daughter shall prick her finger on a spindle and fall down dead!" she screeched, and then rushed out.

"I cannot undo the spell," said the fourth fairy, "but I can soften it. The princess will prick her finger on a spindle, but she will not die. Instead, the princess and everyone within the palace and its grounds will fall into a deep sleep for one hundred years."

The king thanked the fairy and then, to protect his daughter, ordered every spindle in the kingdom to be burned.

The years passed and the princess grew into a beautiful, clever and kind young woman.

One day, the princess decided to explore some rooms in the palace she had never been in before. After a while, she came to a little door at the top of a tall tower. Inside, there was an old woman working at her spinning wheel. The princess didn't know that the woman was really the old fairy in disguise.

"What are you doing?"
the princess asked curiously.

"I'm spinning thread, dear,"
replied the woman.

"Can I try?" asked
the princess.

No sooner had she
touched the spindle
than she pricked her
finger and fell into
a deep sleep.

As she fell asleep, every living thing within the castle walls fell into a deep sleep too.

As time passed, a hedge of thorns sprang up around the palace. It grew higher and thicker every year, until only the tallest towers could be seen above it.

The story of the beautiful princess who lay sleeping within its walls spread throughout the land. She became known as Sleeping Beauty. Many princes tried to break through the thorns to rescue Sleeping Beauty, but none were successful.

Exactly one hundred years after the princess had fallen asleep, a handsome prince, having heard the story of Sleeping Beauty, decided to try and awaken the sleeping princess.

The prince didn't know that the fairy's spell was coming to its end. As he pushed against the thick hedge, every thorn turned into a beautiful rose, and a path magically formed to let him pass.

Soon the prince came to the palace. He saw people and animals asleep in every room.

At last he found the tiny room in the tower where Sleeping Beauty lay. He kissed her gently.

The sleeping princess opened her eyes and smiled. With that one look, they fell in love.

All around the palace, people started waking up. The spell had been broken!

The king called for a huge wedding feast to be prepared, and this time he invited every person, and fairy, in the entire kingdom.

Sleeping Beauty married her handsome prince, and they lived happily ever after.

The Swallow and the Crow

One day, a young swallow landed on a branch next to a wise old crow. The swallow looked down his beak at the crow and said, "I don't think much of your stiff feathers. You should take more pride in your appearance."

The old crow was very angry and was about to fly away, when the swallow continued, "Look at me with my soft, downy feathers. They are what a well-dressed bird needs."

"Those soft feathers of yours might be all right in the spring and summer," the crow replied. "But in the winter you have to fly away to warmer countries. In the winter the trees are covered with ripe berries. I can stay here and enjoy them as I have my stiff, black feathers to keep me warm and dry."

The crow held out his wings. "What use are your fancy feathers then, Swallow?" he asked, before turning away.

And the moral of the story is: Fine-weather friends are not worth much.

The Dog and His Reflection

A hungry dog passed a butcher's shop and spotted a juicy steak lying on the counter. He waited until the butcher went to the back of the shop, then he ran in and stole it.

On his way home, the dog crossed a narrow bridge over a river. As he looked down into the water he saw another dog looking up at him. This dog was also carrying a piece of meat, and it looked even bigger than the one he had!

"I want that steak too," thought the greedy dog. So he jumped into the river to steal the steak from the other dog.

But as he opened his mouth to snatch the steak, the butcher's steak fell from his mouth and sank to the bottom of the river. The other dog vanished in a pool of ripples.

The greedy dog had been fooled by his own reflection, and now he was still hungry and had nothing left to eat!

And the moral of the story is: It doesn't pay to be greedy.

A New Friend

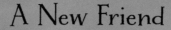

Octopus loved playing with her friends Dolphin and Turtle. Every morning, they played a game called "Sharks" by the old shipwreck near Octopus's cave. In the game, one of the friends would be the shark, while the other two swam away, pretending to be scared.

One morning, Dolphin and Turtle went to meet Octopus, but she wasn't in her cave.

"Where is she?" asked Dolphin, anxiously. "Octopus always waits for us here …"

"Perhaps she's in trouble and needs our help," cried Turtle.

As the two friends set off to find Octopus, they bumped into … a shark!

"Go away!" squeaked Dolphin, shaking with fear.

"Please don't eat us," begged Turtle, starting to cry.

The shark smiled sadly. "I don't want to eat you. I just want to be friends."

He sounded so unhappy that both Turtle and Dolphin felt sorry for him.

"Well," said Turtle, nervously, "maybe you can help us find our friend Octopus."

Shark groaned. "Octopus? Oh, no! I think I scared her away from that cave …"

Turtle and Dolphin glanced at each other. They knew exactly where Octopus would be…at the shipwreck waiting for them! So they swam as fast as they could, with Shark trailing behind.

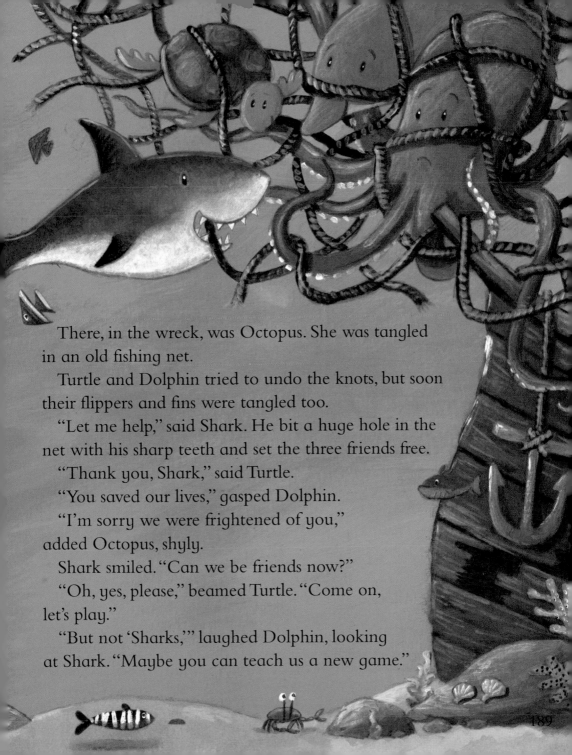

There, in the wreck, was Octopus. She was tangled in an old fishing net.

Turtle and Dolphin tried to undo the knots, but soon their flippers and fins were tangled too.

"Let me help," said Shark. He bit a huge hole in the net with his sharp teeth and set the three friends free.

"Thank you, Shark," said Turtle.

"You saved our lives," gasped Dolphin.

"I'm sorry we were frightened of you," added Octopus, shyly.

Shark smiled. "Can we be friends now?"

"Oh, yes, please," beamed Turtle. "Come on, let's play."

"But not 'Sharks,'" laughed Dolphin, looking at Shark. "Maybe you can teach us a new game."

Five Little Ducks

Five little ducks went swimming one day,
Over the hills and far away.
Mother Duck said, "Quack, quack, quack, quack,"
But only four little ducks came back.

*(Repeat the rhyme, counting down from four little ducks
to one little duck ...)*

One little duck went swimming one day,
Over the hills and far away.
Mother Duck said, "Quack, quack, quack, quack,"
But none of the five little ducks came back.

Mother Duck went swimming one day,
Over the hills and far away.
Mother Duck said, "Quack, quack, quack, quack,"
And five little ducks came swimming back.

190

Hickory Dickory Dock

Hickory dickory dock,
The mouse ran up the clock.
The clock struck one,
And the mouse ran down,
Hickory dickory dock.

Marking Time

Tick! Tock!
That's the clock
Marking time for me.
Every tick
And every tock,
Sets each second free.

Old Mother Hubbard

Old Mother Hubbard
Went to the cupboard,
To get her poor doggie a bone.
But when she got there
The cupboard was bare,
And her poor little doggie had none.

I Love My Daddy

One day, Little Squirrel wanted to show Daddy Squirrel all the things he could do.

"What shall we do first?" said Daddy.

"Digging!" said Little Squirrel excitedly, as he dug and dug, with his little tail wagging.

"Well done!" said Daddy. But suddenly, Little Squirrel's tail stopped wagging.

"Help, Daddy! I'm stuck!"

Daddy Squirrel helped Little Squirrel wriggle out of the hole, and gave him a hug.

"You are a good digger!" said Daddy. "What shall we play next?"

"Climbing!" said Little Squirrel, and he climbed as high as he could go.

"Well done!" said Daddy. But suddenly Little Squirrel closed his eyes tightly …

"Help, Daddy! I'm stuck!"

Daddy Squirrel helped Little Squirrel climb down and gave him a hug.

"You are a good climber!" said Daddy. "What shall we play next?"

"Jumping!" said Little Squirrel, and he jumped with a big smile on his face. But suddenly Little Squirrel stopped smiling, and … SPLAT! He was in the mud.

"Help, Daddy! I'm stuck again!"

Daddy Squirrel helped Little Squirrel out of the sticky patch of mud and gave him a hug.

"You are good at jumping!" said Daddy.

But Little Squirrel shook his head sadly …

"I can't do anything!" cried Little Squirrel. "I always get stuck!"

Daddy Squirrel lifted Little Squirrel onto his shoulders.

"Let's play together," he said. "Let's run!"

Little Squirrel held on tightly as they whooshed through the woods.

"Yippee!" he shouted.

"Let's climb!" said Daddy Squirrel. Little Squirrel kept his eyes open wide as they reached the top of a tree.

"Wheeee!" he shouted.

"And now," said Daddy Squirrel, "let's jump!"

SPLAT!

"Oh, help!" cried Daddy Squirrel. "Now I'm stuck!"

Little Squirrel giggled as he helped his daddy out of the sticky mud.

"You can do everything, Little Squirrel!" said Daddy proudly. "You can even save a Daddy Squirrel!"

Little Squirrel grinned. "I love playing with you … and I love my daddy!" he shouted, and they raced home happily together.

The Rainbow's End

How did it get there, so pretty and bright?
It must be a magical fairy light.
Shimmering colors, up so high,
A beautiful rainbow, painting the sky!

Is it a wonderful fairyland slide,
Where pixies and fairies can go for a ride?
I'd like to follow it, because I'm told
At the rainbow's end is a pot of gold!

Itsy Bitsy Spider

Itsy Bitsy Spider
Climbed up the water spout.
Down came the rain
And washed the spider out.

Out came the sun
And dried up all the rain.
And the Itsy Bitsy Spider
Climbed up the spout again.

Gee Up, Teddy

Gee up, Teddy,
Don't you stop!
Ride on the hobbyhorse,
Clippety clop!
Clippety clopping,
Round and round,
Giddy up,
We're toybox bound!

Round and Round the Garden

Round and round the garden
Like a teddy bear.
One step, two steps,
Tickly under there!

Here We Go Round the Mulberry Bush

Here we go round the mulberry bush,
The mulberry bush, the mulberry bush,
Here we go round the mulberry bush,
On a cold and frosty morning.

The Biggest Squeak in the World

Freddie couldn't squeak. Squeaking doesn't matter if you're a dog or a cat, but unfortunately Freddie was a mouse. And mice are supposed to squeak.

"All my friends can squeak," he said. "What's wrong with me?"

"You're just not ready yet," said his grandfather. "It will happen when the time is right."

Later that day, Freddie was moping outside the mouse hole when suddenly … HISS! A huge, hungry cat came springing toward him!

Freddie opened his mouth to yell for help—and instead let out an enormous SQUEAK! Every single mouse in the town heard it. Dogs heard it. Even humans heard it. The cat leaped into the air and all its fur stood on end. Then it shot away in terror.

When the other mice heard about the cat, they gave Freddie a big cheer.

"That's why your squeak took a long time to come," his grandfather laughed. "It's the biggest squeak in the world!"

Achoo!

Mouse's eyes filled up with water,
His little nose started to twitch,
A tingling tickled his whiskers,
And then his knees started to itch.

He got a bad case of the hiccups,
Then threw back his head in a sneeze,
And he said, "I'm feeling really bad,
It's just I'm allergic to cheese!"

The Gingerbread Man

There was once a little old woman and a little old man. One morning, the little old woman decided to bake a gingerbread man. She mixed all the ingredients together, rolled out the dough, cut out the gingerbread man, then popped him in the oven to bake.

But when the little old woman opened the oven door, the gingerbread man jumped up and ran away.

"Stop!" cried the little old woman.

"We want to eat you!" cried the little old man. And they ran after the gingerbread man. But he was too fast.

"Run, run, as fast as you can. You can't catch me, I'm the gingerbread man!" he sang.

Then he darted into a field, passing a pig, a cow, and a horse. They all wanted to eat him, too!

"I've run away from a little old woman and a little old man, and I can run away from you!" he told the animals. And he sang, "Run, run, as fast as you can. You can't catch me, I'm the gingerbread man!"

The little old woman, the little old man, the pig, the cow, and the horse ran and ran, but none of them could catch the gingerbread man.

After a while, the gingerbread man reached a river.

"How will I get across?" he cried.

A sly fox saw the gingerbread man, and licked his lips.

"Jump onto my back and I will take you across the river," he told the gingerbread man.

So the gingerbread man jumped onto the fox's back, and the fox began to swim across the river.

After a while, the fox cried, "You're too heavy for my back. Jump onto my nose." So the gingerbread man scrambled onto his nose.

But as soon as they reached the riverbank, the fox flipped the gingerbread man up into the air, and he fell straight into his open jaws. The fox snapped his mouth shut and gobbled him up.

And that was the end of the gingerbread man!

The Giant Squid's Garden

Eric the dolphin lived in the deepest part of the ocean with his mother and his two sisters, Erin and Eva. One day, he woke up with a playful, wriggly sort of feeling in his belly.

"It's just the sort of day for mischief," he said.

Erin and Eva, who were very well-behaved dolphins, didn't like the sound of that at all.

"Let's go and leap through the waves with our friends," said Eva.

But Eric shook his head. He had suddenly thought of a brilliant idea.

"I'm going to look for sea slugs in the giant squid's garden," he said.

The giant squid was very bad tempered, and he didn't like the little dolphins eating the sea slugs from his garden. If he saw them, he always tried to catch them in his huge tentacles.

Eric dived down to the giant squid's garden and swam through the colorful coral beds. Then he spotted some juicy sea slugs just outside the giant squid's cave entrance. He swam closer and snapped one up.

"You pesky dolphin!" roared a voice. It was the giant squid!

The giant squid's long tentacles whipped out of
the cave and wrapped around Eric's tail.

"Help!" squealed Eric. "Let me go!"

He wriggled around, and suddenly the giant squid
started to giggle.

"Stop it!" he roared. "You're tickling me with your tail!"

Eric wriggled even more, and the giant squid was soon
laughing helplessly. His grip loosened and Eric darted free,
swimming away as fast as he could.

"And don't come back!" yelled the giant squid, shaking
his tentacles.

Erin and Eva gasped when they heard about Eric's adventure.

"Of course you'll never go there again," said Eva.

"Of course not," agreed Eric, with a twinkle in his eye.
"Not unless I can make the giant squid laugh again!"

Ten Little Teddies

Ten little teddies, standing in a line,
One of them went fishing, so then there were nine.
Nine little teddies, marching through a gate,
One stopped to tie his shoe, so then there were eight.

Eight little teddies, floating up in heaven,
One fell down and broke his crown, so then there were seven.
Seven little teddies, doing magic tricks,
One made himself disappear, so then there were six.

Six little teddies, about to take a dive,
One of them was scared of heights, so then there were five.
Five little teddies, running on the shore,
One went surfing in the waves, so then there were four.

Four little teddies, eating cakes for tea,
One of them was feeling sick, so then there were three.
Three little teddies, heading for the zoo,
One thought he'd take the bus, so then there were two.

Two little teddies, playing in the sun,
One of them got sunburned, so then there was one.
One little teddy, who's had lots of fun,
It's time for him to go to sleep, so now there are none.

Midnight Fun

Just as midnight's striking,
When everyone's asleep,
Teddies yawn and stretch and shake,
And out of warm beds creep.

They sneak out from their houses,
And gather in the dark,
Then skip along the empty streets,
Heading for the park.

And there beneath the moonlight,
They tumble down the slides,
They swoosh up high upon the swings,
And play on all the rides.

And when the sun comes peeping,
They rush home to their beds,
And snuggle down as children wake,
To cuddle with their teds!

203

I Had a Little Hobby Horse

I had a little hobby horse,
And it was dapple gray.
Its head was made of pea-straw,
Its tail was made of hay.
I sold it to an old woman
For a copper groat,
And I'll not sing my song again
Without another coat.

Horsie, Horsie

Horsie, horsie, don't you stop,
Just let your feet go clippety clop,
Your tail goes swish,
And the wheels go round,
Giddy up, you're homeward bound!

The Lion and the Unicorn

The lion and the unicorn were fighting for the crown,
The lion beat the unicorn all around the town.
Some gave them white bread,
And some gave them brown,
Some gave them plum cake,
And drummed them out of town.

Ride a Cock Horse

Ride a cock horse to Banbury Cross
To see a fine lady upon a white horse.
With rings on her fingers and bells on her toes,
She shall have music wherever she goes.

Mary Had a Little Lamb

Mary had a little lamb,
Its fleece was white as snow,
And everywhere that Mary went
The lamb was sure to go.
It followed her to school one day,
Which was against the rule.
It made the children laugh and play
To see a lamb at school.

Roly and Poly

Roly and Poly were polar bears. They lived in the cold, frozen north where they liked to play in the ice and the snow all day long.

One morning, the little bears started to feel tired.

"Let's sit down for a rest!" sighed Roly.

Poly pointed to a big, gray rock sticking out of the sea. "That looks like a brilliant place to sit!" he said.

So Roly and Poly jumped onto the big, gray shape, and settled down for a rest. They yawned and stretched, and in no time at all fell fast asleep.

The sky grew dark and the stars began to twinkle. As the little bears snored gently, and the big, silvery moon rose high in the sky, the gray rock suddenly started to move, slipping out into the cold sea.

In fact, the gray rock was not a rock at all. It was a humpback whale, who had just woken up and had no idea that two little bears were fast asleep on her back. The whale dived down into the murky depths, and icy-cold water rushed up around her.

"row!" yelled Roly and Poly, waking up in the sea.

The whale heard the bears' loud cries and came back up to the surface.

"What are you doing out here in the night?" she asked.

"We don't know!" said Roly and Poly together, and they started to cry.

"Well, I'd better take you home," said the whale kindly. "Climb on."

"Your back looks like the gray rock that we sat on," said Roly.

"I think your back IS the gray rock that we sat on," said Poly.

Roly and Poly enjoyed their moonlight ride, and before long they were home again, safe with their mom. The whale swam off, waving goodbye with her huge tail.

"Goodbye and goodnight!" sighed Roly and Poly, as they drifted off to sleep, dreaming of their big adventure.

Curious Kitten

Misty was a curious kitten. One day, she was watching Mrs. Duck lead her waddling ducklings across the yard.

"I wonder what it's like being a duck," she thought.

She scurried along behind the ducklings, trying her best to quack, but all she could manage was a strange "Meow-ack!"

When the ducklings nibbled the grass on the riverbank, Misty tried a little herself, but it made her cough.

Then the ducklings followed their mother into the lake for a swim.

"That looks easy," cried Misty, and she jumped in with a big SPLASH! But swimming wasn't easy for a kitten at all!

Luckily, Scratch the sheepdog was nearby. He leaped in and gently pulled Misty out, using his teeth on the scruff of her neck.

"Thanks," said Misty. "I thought it would be fun to be a duck, but I think I'll stick to being a kitten."

She had just sat down to lick her fur dry, when she had an idea—perhaps she could try being a sheepdog instead!

Nippy Snippy

Eeeny, meeny, miney, mo,
Here comes Crab to pinch your toe!
Shout out loud and he'll let go—
Eeeny, meeny, miney, mo!

Nippy, snippy, snappy, snip,
Be careful when you take a dip,
Or Crab will catch you in his grip!
Nippy, snippy, snappy, snip!

Snow White

Once there was a queen who longed for a daughter. As she sat sewing by her window one winter's day, she pricked her finger on the needle. As blood fell from her finger she thought, "I wish I had a daughter with lips as red as blood, hair as black as ebony wood, and skin as white as the snow outside!"

Before long, the queen gave birth to a baby girl with blood-red lips, ebony hair, and skin as white as snow. She called her Snow White.

Sadly, the queen died, and the king married again. His new wife was beautiful, but vain.

She had a magic mirror, and every day she looked into it and asked:

"Mirror, mirror, on the wall,
Who is the fairest of them all?"

And every day the mirror replied:

"You, O Queen, are the fairest of them all."

But Snow White became more and more beautiful every day. One morning, when the queen asked the mirror who was the fairest, the mirror replied:

*"You, O Queen, are fair, it's true.
But young Snow White is fairer than you."*

Furious, the queen told her huntsman, "Take Snow White into the forest and kill her!"

The huntsman led Snow White deep into the forest, but could not bear to hurt her. "Run far away from here," he said.

As darkness fell, Snow White came upon a little cottage. She knocked softly on the door, but there was no answer, so she let herself in. Inside, Snow White found a table and seven tiny chairs.

Upstairs there were seven little beds.

Snow White lay down on the seventh bed and fell fast asleep.

She awoke to find seven little men staring at her in amazement.

"Who are you?" she asked.

"We are the seven dwarves who live here," said one dwarf. "Who are you?"

"I am Snow White," she replied, and she told them her sad story.

"You can stay with us," said the eldest dwarf, kindly.

Every day, the seven dwarves went to work while Snow White cooked and cleaned the cottage.

"Don't open the door to anyone," they told her, worried the wicked queen might find her.

Meanwhile, when the wicked queen asked her mirror once more who was the fairest that day, it replied:

> *"You, O Queen, are fair, it's true,*
> *But Snow White is still fairer than you.*
> *Deep in the forest with seven little men*
> *Snow White is living in a cozy den."*

The queen was furious and vowed to kill Snow White herself. So she added poison to a juicy apple, then set off to the forest, disguised as a peddler woman.

"Try my juicy apples!" she called out, knocking on the door of the seven dwarves' cottage.

Snow White remembered the dwarves' warning, so she just opened the window to take a look.

When the queen offered Snow White an apple, she took a big bite. The poisoned piece got stuck in her throat, and she fell to the ground.

When the seven dwarves returned, they were heartbroken to find their beloved Snow White dead. They couldn't bear to bury her, so they put her in a glass coffin and placed it in the forest, where they took turns watching over her.

One day, a prince rode by and saw Snow White. The dwarves told him her sad story.

"Please let me take her away," begged the prince. The dwarves could see he loved Snow White, and they agreed to let her go.

As the prince's servants lifted the coffin, one of them stumbled, jolting the poisoned apple from Snow White's throat, and she came back to life.

When Snow White saw the handsome prince, she fell deeply in love with him.

They soon married, and lived happily ever after together with the dwarves.

Jungle Ballet

Milly Monkey didn't like the dark. She snuggled up on Granny Monkey's knee and tried not to look at it, but it was all around her.

"The dark isn't scary," said Granny Monkey. "Don't you know what happens at night when the stars come out?"

Milly shook her head.

"Sometimes, the jungle puts on a magical ballet," whispered Granny Monkey. "Little lights twirl and dance, but you can only see them if you're in bed."

Milly longed to see the ballet. Bravely, she climbed into bed and said good night. Then Granny Monkey began to sing a beautiful lullaby. Her song called all the fireflies in the jungle, and they danced around Milly's head until she fell asleep.

Next day, Milly told Granny Monkey, "You were right. Dark isn't scary. Dark is magical."

And Granny Monkey gave a wise old smile!

Brave Amy

Amy the ostrich wasn't like her ostrich friends. They were afraid of everything—from loud noises to sandstorms. And whenever anything scared them, they buried their heads in the sand. But Amy never did.

Amy dreamed of having adventures, but her friends just laughed.

"Ostriches don't go traveling," they said. "It's much too scary."

One evening, the ostriches heard a big noise drifting across the plain. BANG! BANG! TOOT! TOOT! Of course, they all buried their heads in the sand. But not Amy—she stood up straight.

"I'm not scared," she said bravely.

In the evening light, she saw a traveling band marching toward her. They were playing drums and trumpets. BANG! BANG! TOOT! TOOT! And they all looked very happy.

"I like your band," Amy said shyly.

"Then join us!" said a camel with a drum.

Amy looked at her friends with their heads buried in the sand and she knew what she wanted to do.

Now, Amy has great adventures with the marching band, and she bangs the loudest drum of all!

The Perfect Pet

Emily was visiting her friend Ethan's farm to choose a puppy. Most of the puppies bounded around the barn, barking and jumping on each other. But one puppy gently pressed against Emily's legs and licked her knees.

"I like this one," said Emily, looking at the puppy's cute brown fur.

"Are you sure?" asked Ethan. "Rusty doesn't chase sticks and run around like the other puppies."

Rusty's ears drooped, and he pressed closer to Emily. It was true he wasn't like the others. But Emily looked down at his sad eyes and smiled at him.

"Look, he's so gentle and kind," said Emily, tickling Rusty's ears. "He's the perfect pet for me!"

Rusty's heart leaped with happiness, and he wagged his little tail. And Emily knew that she had found the most perfect pet in the whole, wide world.

The Secret Cat Circus

Every morning, when they went to work, Jessie's owners left her dozing in the sunniest corner of the garden. They thought she was a very sleepy cat, but Jessie had a secret. As soon as they had gone, Jessie pulled on a sparkly costume and went to work too … at the cat circus hidden at the bottom of their garden!

"Gather around!" the tabby circus master shouted to the growing crowd. "Come and see the best tightrope-walking cat in the whole wide world!"

The crowd gasped as Jessie walked the tightrope, balancing a fish on her nose and juggling balls of string.

By five o'clock the circus show was over and Jessie pulled off her costume, settling down to doze in the sun for when her owners came home.

"That cat could sleep all day!" Jessie's owners cried each evening.

Little did they know of her performing talent—or where the sparkles in her fur came from!

Town Mouse and Country Mouse

Once there were two little mice. One lived in the town, and the other in the country.

One day, Town Mouse visited Country Mouse's home. It was small and dark—not at all like Town Mouse's home.

After lunch, the two friends went for a walk. First, they strolled into a field.

"Moo!"

"What was that?" asked Town Mouse nervously.

"Just a cow," replied his friend.

So they continued walking toward a peaceful pond.

"Hiss!"

"What was that?" asked Town Mouse, quivering from nose to tail.

"Just a goose," replied his friend.

So the two mice strolled on into a shady wood.

"Twit-twoo!"

"What was that?" yelped Town Mouse.

"An owl!" cried Country Mouse. "Quick! Run before it eats you!"

So they ran until they found a hedge to hide in.

"I don't like the country!" Town Mouse cried. "Come with me to the town. It's much better!" So they went.

Town Mouse's home was huge and grand—not at all like Country Mouse's home.

After dinner, the friends went for a walk, passing some shops on the way.

"Beep-beep!"

"What's that?" asked Country Mouse fearfully.

"Just a car," said his friend.

The mice continued strolling down a wide road.

"Nee-nah! Nee-nah!"

"What's that?" asked Country Mouse, his whiskers twitching.

"Just a fire engine," his friend replied.

As they pitter-pattered home, they passed a pretty garden.

"Meow!"

"What's that?" squeaked Country Mouse.

"A cat!" cried Town Mouse. "Quick! Run before it eats you!"

So they ran all the way back to Town Mouse's house.

"I don't like the town! I'm going home," cried Country Mouse.

"But what about that owl?" asked Town Mouse.

"It doesn't scare me!" cried Country Mouse. "What about that cat?"

"It doesn't scare me!" cried Town Mouse.

The two mice knew they would never agree. So they shook hands and went their separate ways.

And they lived happily ever after, each in his own way.

Underpants Wonderpants

Is it an eagle? Is it a plane?
No—it's Underpants Wonderpants to the rescue again!
Whenever you need him, in sun, snow, or shower,
He'll sort out your problems with UNDERPANTS POWER!

"Elephant sat on our nest!" grumbles Mouse.
"No problem!" says Wonderpants.
ZAP! An underpants house!

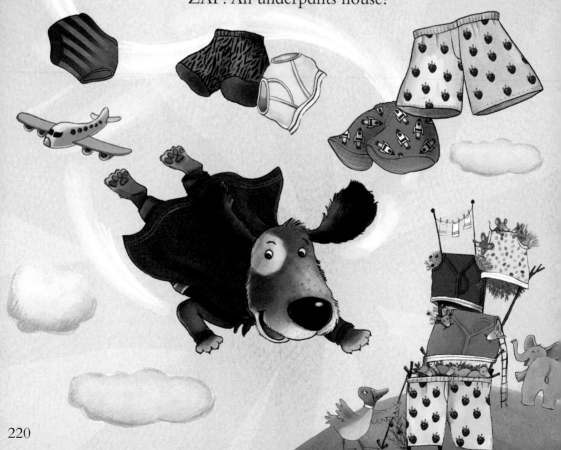

Kangaroo cries,
"I've been itching all night!"
ZAP! In this hammock, the insects can't bite!

Polar Bear Cub can't keep up in the storm.
ZAP! Thanks to Wonderpants she's cozy and warm!

The fisherman's ripped a big hole in his net.
ZAP! "Thank you, Wonderpants! It's my biggest catch yet!"

"Help!" cries the queen.
It's so far to the ground—
Wonderpants Pantachute helps her
land safe and sound!

Wonderpants zooms to the river,
and in a great swoop—
he puts out the fire with his
SUPER-PANT SCOOP!

But that's not the end of his super-pants day …
An alien spaceship is heading this way!
The creatures are grinning and shaking with mirth:
"As soon as we land we'll take over the Earth!"

But imagine the look on each alien's face
When a Wonderpants sling sends them—ZAP!—back to space!
The people all cheer as they watch from afar:
"Wonderpants saved us all—he's our SUPER-PANTS STAR!"

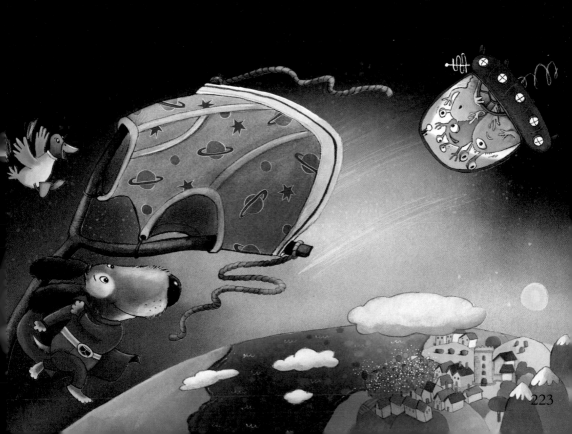

Row, Row, Row Your Boat

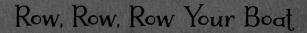

Row, row, row your boat
Gently down the stream.
Merrily, merrily, merrily, merrily,
Life is but a dream.

One, Two, Three, Four, Five

One, two, three, four, five,
Once I caught a fish alive.
Six, seven, eight, nine, ten,
Then I let it go again.
Why did you let it go?
Because it bit my finger so.
Which finger did it bite?
This little finger on the right.

Pussy Cat, Pussy Cat

Pussy cat, pussy cat,
Where have you been?
I've been to London
To visit the Queen.
Pussy cat, pussy cat,
What did you there?
I frightened a little mouse
Under her chair.

Ding Dong Bell

Ding dong bell,
Pussy cat's in the well.
Who put her in?
Little Johnny Flynn.
Who pulled her out?
Little Tommy Stout.
What a naughty boy was that
To try to drown poor pussy cat,
Who never did any harm
But killed all the mice
In the farmer's barn!

225

Peacock's Birthday

It was Peacock's birthday, and he was having a party in the garden. He spent all morning brushing his feathers and polishing his beak.

"This is going to be the best birthday ever," said Peacock. "Everyone will say how handsome I look. Everyone will admire my beautiful feathers."

When his peacock friends arrived, they all said "Happy birthday!" and gave him presents. Then they went to play hide and seek at the muddy end of the yard.

"Come and join in," they called to Peacock. But Peacock didn't want to get dirty.

Peacock's mother filled up the wading pool, and everyone splashed around in the water.

"It's lovely and cool!" they called to Peacock. But Peacock didn't want to get his beak wet.

Peacock's father put on some music and the guests started a game of musical chairs.

"Play with us, Peacock!" they called. But Peacock didn't want to mess up his sleek feathers.

Peacock strutted around the yard with all his feathers on display. He knew that he looked splendid, but he felt a bit lonely. All the other peacocks seemed to be having a much better time. Then his father came over.

"You know, feathers can be cleaned," he said. "But if you miss out on having fun with your friends, you will always feel sorry about it."

Peacock thought very hard. He liked to look smart … but he liked his friends even more.

"Wait for me!" he yelled.

He dashed across the yard to join the game, and his father smiled. Soon, Peacock was covered with water and mud, and his feathers were sticking up in the air. He was messy and mucky, and it was the happiest birthday he had ever had!

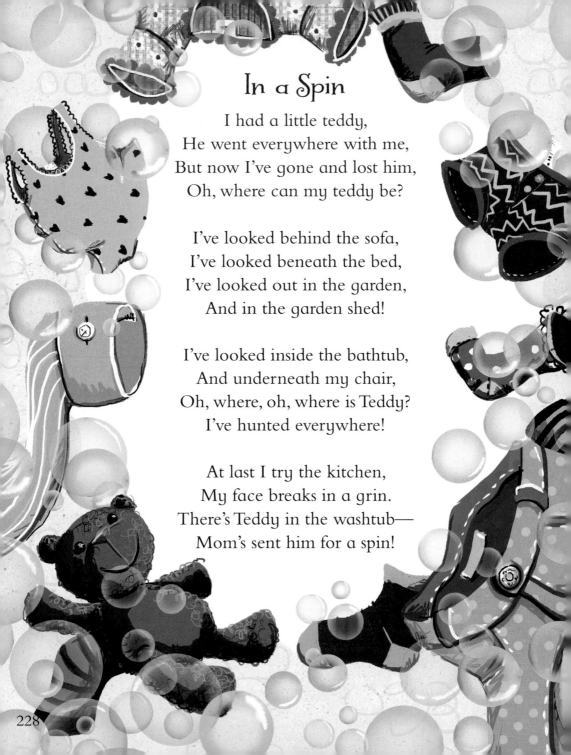

In a Spin

I had a little teddy,
He went everywhere with me,
But now I've gone and lost him,
Oh, where can my teddy be?

I've looked behind the sofa,
I've looked beneath the bed,
I've looked out in the garden,
And in the garden shed!

I've looked inside the bathtub,
And underneath my chair,
Oh, where, oh, where is Teddy?
I've hunted everywhere!

At last I try the kitchen,
My face breaks in a grin.
There's Teddy in the washtub—
Mom's sent him for a spin!

The Egg

Little Parrot lived in a nest with Mommy and a big pink speckled egg.

"I'm going to find some food," Mommy told her one day. "You must look after the egg until I return."

Little Parrot watched the egg for a very long time.

Then she wobbled it around to make it comfortable, and wrapped her wings around it to keep it warm.

"I'm very good at looking after eggs," she squawked, feeling pleased with herself.

Just then, Little Parrot heard a tap, tap, tapping noise coming from the egg, then … CRACK!

"Oh, no, I've broken it!" she cried. "Mommy will be mad!"

But when Mommy returned, she wasn't angry at all.

"Look," she said, as a tiny baby parrot popped out of the broken eggshell. "You took care of the egg perfectly. Now it's hatched and you've got a new baby sister to play with!"

Jack and the Beanstalk

There was once a young boy named Jack, who lived with his mother. They had no money and nothing left to eat.

"We have no choice but to sell Bluebell, our old cow," said Jack's mother. "Take her to market and sell her for a good price."

So Jack set off with Bluebell.

Before long, he met an old man, who asked, "Are you selling that fine cow?"

"Yes," Jack replied.

"Well, I'll give you these magic beans for her," said the man. "They don't look much, but if you plant them, you will soon be rich!"

Jack liked the sound of that, and he gave Bluebell to the man.

When Jack showed his mother the beans she was very angry.

"Silly boy! Go to your room!" she cried, throwing the beans out of the window.

The next morning, when Jack woke up, his room was strangely dark. He looked out of his window and saw a plant so tall that he couldn't see the top of it.

"It must be a magic beanstalk!" he cried.

Jack started to climb. When he reached the top, he saw a giant house. Jack's tummy was rumbling with hunger, so he knocked on the enormous door, and a giant woman answered.

"Please may I have some breakfast?" asked Jack.

"You'll BE breakfast if my husband sees you!" said the woman.

But Jack begged and pleaded, and at last the giant's wife let him in. She gave him some bread and milk and hid him in a cupboard.

Soon Jack heard loud footsteps and felt the cupboard shake.

"Fee-fi-fo-fum! I smell the blood of an Englishman!" roared the giant.

"Don't be silly," the giant's wife said. "You smell the sausages I've cooked for your breakfast."

When the giant had finished eating, he counted the hundreds of huge gold coins in his treasure chest. But the counting soon sent him to sleep.

As quick as a flash, Jack grabbed the coins, ran out of the house, and climbed down the beanstalk.

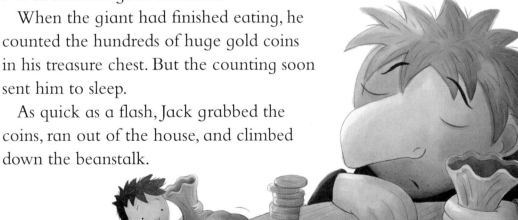

His mother was so happy to see the gold. "Clever boy! We'll never be poor again!" she laughed.

But soon Jack and his mother had spent all the money, so the boy climbed the beanstalk again. He knocked on the huge door and begged the giant's wife to give him some food. At last she let him in.

After eating his breakfast, Jack hid in the cupboard just as the giant arrived home for lunch.

When he had finished eating, his wife brought him his pet hen.

"Lay!" he bellowed, and the hen laid a golden egg. It laid ten eggs before the giant started to snore. Jack couldn't believe his luck, so he picked up the hen and ran.

His mother beamed when she saw the hen lay a golden egg.

"We will never be hungry again," she said.

But even though Jack and his mother were rich, the boy decided to climb the beanstalk one more time.

Jack knew the giant's wife wouldn't be happy to see him, so he sneaked in when she wasn't looking and hid in the cupboard.

When the giant came home, his wife brought him his magic harp.

"Play!" he roared, and the harp played such sweet music the giant soon fell asleep.

Jack saw his chance and grabbed the harp. As he ran, the harp cried out, "Master! Help!"

The giant woke up and began to chase Jack down the beanstalk.

"Mother, fetch the ax!" Jack yelled as he reached the ground. He chopped at the beanstalk with all his might. CREAK! GROAN! The giant quickly climbed back to the top just before the beanstalk crashed to the ground.

When his mother heard the harp play, she laughed and hugged Jack tightly.

"My clever boy!" she said. And the two of them lived happily ever after.

Dinosaur Attack!

Felix the dinosaur was the smallest dinosaur in his herd, but there was one thing he could do better than all the others. He could run very, very fast.

"Felix, slow down!" the other dinosaurs said to him every day as he whizzed past.

But Felix wouldn't listen.

One day, the dinosaurs were munching leaves in their camp when they heard a loud THUMP! THUMP!

"It's T. rex!" the chief dinosaur shouted. "Hide!"

All the dinosaurs did exactly as they were told … all except Felix, who had an idea. There was a cliff nearby, and at the bottom was a large lake. If T. rex chased after him, perhaps Felix could lead him off the cliff!

THUMP! THUMP! THUMP! T. rex stomped into the camp. Felix took a deep breath and jumped out in front of him.

"Silly old T. rex!" he shouted, and blew a loud raspberry.

T. rex bared his teeth.

"No one blows raspberries at me!" he roared, and he started to chase Felix.

Felix ran faster than he had ever run before, all the way to the cliff—and T. rex got closer and closer.

Just before Felix reached the edge, he grabbed hold of a bush and stopped sharp. But T. rex was too big to stop himself in time, and he ran straight off the cliff and landed in the lake.

SPLASH!

"Good riddance!" said Felix, peering over at T. rex spluttering in the lake below.

All the other dinosaurs in the herd slowly came out of their hiding places.

"Felix, you're a hero!" said the chief.

"No, I'm not," said Felix in a modest voice. "I'm just a very fast runner."

"Well, we're very proud of you!" the chief said. "And we'll never complain about you running again!"

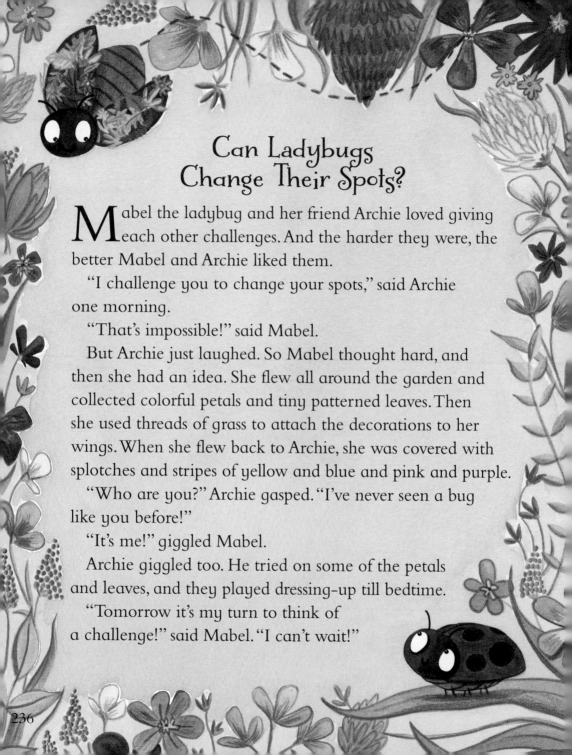

Can Ladybugs Change Their Spots?

Mabel the ladybug and her friend Archie loved giving each other challenges. And the harder they were, the better Mabel and Archie liked them.

"I challenge you to change your spots," said Archie one morning.

"That's impossible!" said Mabel.

But Archie just laughed. So Mabel thought hard, and then she had an idea. She flew all around the garden and collected colorful petals and tiny patterned leaves. Then she used threads of grass to attach the decorations to her wings. When she flew back to Archie, she was covered with splotches and stripes of yellow and blue and pink and purple.

"Who are you?" Archie gasped. "I've never seen a bug like you before!"

"It's me!" giggled Mabel.

Archie giggled too. He tried on some of the petals and leaves, and they played dressing-up till bedtime.

"Tomorrow it's my turn to think of a challenge!" said Mabel. "I can't wait!"

There Was an Old Woman Who Swallowed a Fly

There was an old woman who swallowed a fly,
I don't know why she swallowed a fly!

She swallowed a spider to catch the fly,
It wriggled and jiggled and tickled inside her.

She swallowed a cat to catch the spider,
She swallowed a dog to catch the cat,
She swallowed a cow to catch the dog,
She swallowed a horse to catch the cow.

She's filled up now!

Five Fat Peas

Five fat peas in a pea-pod pressed,
One grew, two grew, so did all the rest.
They grew, and grew, and did not stop,
Until one day, the pod went POP!

Catch It If You Can

Mix a pancake,
Beat a pancake,
Put it in a pan.
Cook a pancake,
Toss a pancake,
Catch it if you can!

Dibbity, Dibbity, Dibbity, Doe

Dibbity, dibbity, dibbity, doe,
Give me a pancake, and I'll go.
Dibbity, dibbity, dibbity, ditter,
Please give me a lovely fritter.

Five Fat Sausages

Five fat sausages sizzling in the pan,
All of a sudden one went BANG!
Four fat sausages sizzling in the pan,
All of a sudden one went BANG!
Three fat sausages sizzling in the pan,
All of a sudden one went BANG!
Two fat sausages sizzling in the pan,
All of a sudden one went BANG!
One fat sausage sizzling in the pan,
All of a sudden it went BANG!

Pat-a-Cake, Pat-a-Cake

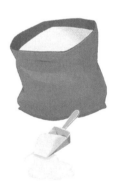

Pat-a-cake, pat-a-cake, baker's man,
Bake me a cake as fast as you can.
Pat it and prick it and mark it with B,
And put it in the oven for Baby and me!
For Baby and me, for Baby and me,
Put it in the oven for Baby and me.

Bunny Loves to Read

Buster Bunny loved books. He read stories of princes … and pirates … and witches and wizards … he read books about trains … and dinosaurs.

One day, Buster's friends came over.

"Hi Buster!" they said. "Are you coming out to play?"

"Sure," said Buster with a smile, "when I've finished my book. It's all about pirates!"

"You've always got your nose in a book!" said his sister Bella. "Hopscotch is more fun!"

"Books are boring!" croaked Francine the frog. "Why read books when you can play leapfrog?"

"Racing each other is even more fun," said Max the mouse.

"Don't listen to them, Buster," said Sam the squirrel. "I think books are the best!"

"Really?" asked Buster.

"Yes," said Sam, smiling. "Books are the best—for nibbling!"

"Hey!" laughed Buster.

Then Bella said, "Come on, let's leave Buster with his dumb old books and play outside!"

But it was raining. The friends looked out of the window gloomily.

"Why don't you read some of my books?" asked Buster, bringing out a big box.

"We don't want to look at books," said Sam grumpily. "We're only waiting for the rain to stop."

Buster took a book out of the box.

"There's a big thunderstorm in this story," said Buster. "It's all about pirates hunting for buried treasure."

"Buried treasure?" asked Sam. "Like nuts and acorns? Yum!"

"Not exactly," replied Buster. "But it's very exciting. Take a look."

"I guess there's nothing better to do," sighed Sam.

"Frogs really hate being stuck inside!" grumbled Francine.

"This book is about a prince who turns into a frog," Buster said.

"Good for him," said Francine. "Does he turn back into a prince?"

"Why don't you read it and find out?" smiled Buster.

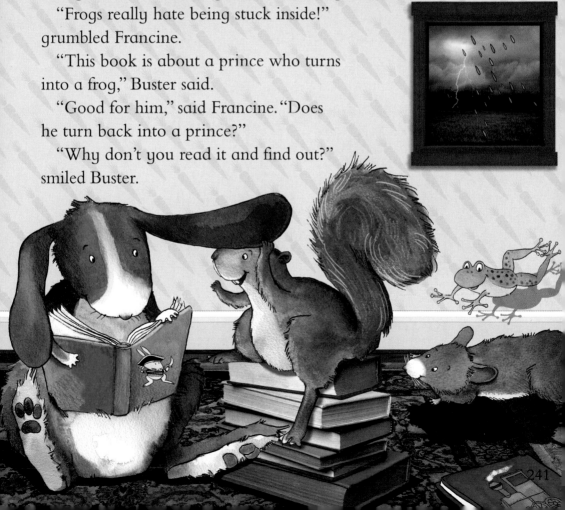

241

"Being cooped up inside is making me sleepy," said Max.

Buster gave Max a book. "The princess in this story goes to sleep for a hundred years!" he said.

"Really? Wow! How does she wake up?"

"Read it and see!" said Buster.

"Well, okay, but I might fall asleep before I finish it!"

"I'm bored! I'm going to get a cookie," said Bella. "Hey, Buster, your box is in my way!"

"Can't you just step over it?"

"Only if I take a giant step," said Bella.

"Just like a dinosaur!" said Buster. "Some of them were bigger than a house!"

Buster looked out the window. "Hey, it's stopped raining!" he cried. "Who's coming out to play?"

"Shh! I'm still reading. The pirates haven't found the treasure yet!" said Sam.

"And the prince is still a frog!" croaked Francine.

"And the brave knight is still searching for the sleeping princess!" cried Max.

"And I've just gotten to a good part about Tyrannosaurus rex!" laughed Bella.

"So what do you want to play outside?" asked Buster when the friends had all finished reading. "Hopscotch? Leapfrog? Tag?"

"Let's pretend we can do magic spells. If you give me a kiss, I'll turn into a princess!" said Francine.

"Ugh! No thanks!" laughed Sam. "Let's play pirates!"

"Look out," said Bella. "I'm a Tyrannosaurus! ROOAAR!"

"I'm off to find the enchanted princess!" cried Max.

They played pirates and dinosaurs and princes and princesses until it was time to go home.

"Do you have any other books about dinosaurs?" asked Bella.

"Sure!" said Buster.

"What about frogs?" asked Francine.

"Yes," said Buster. "And toads too."

"Anything else about witches and magic?" asked Max.

"Loads!"

"Can I borrow another pirate story?" Sam asked.

"Of course you can," laughed Buster, "as long as you promise not to eat it!"

Georgie Porgie

Georgie Porgie, pudding and pie,
Kissed the girls, and made them cry.
When the boys came out to play,
Georgie Porgie ran away.

Yankee Doodle

Yankee Doodle went to town,
Riding on a pony;
He stuck a feather in his cap
And called it macaroni.

One Misty, Moisty Morning

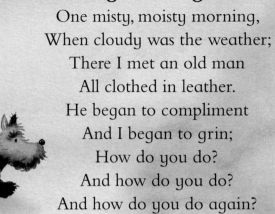

One misty, moisty morning,
When cloudy was the weather;
There I met an old man
All clothed in leather.
He began to compliment
And I began to grin;
How do you do?
And how do you do?
And how do you do again?

A-Tisket, A-Tasket

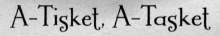

A-tisket, a-tasket,
A green and yellow basket.
I wrote a letter to my love,
And on the way I dropped it.
I dropped it, I dropped it,
And on the way I dropped it.
A little boy picked it up,
And put it in his pocket.

Cobbler, Cobbler

Cobbler, cobbler, mend my shoe,
Get it done by half past two.
Half past two is much too late!
Get it done by half past eight.

Rumpelstiltskin

Long ago, a poor miller was so desperate to impress the king that he told him his daughter could spin straw into gold!

"This I must see," said the king.

The next day, at the palace, the king led the girl to a room filled with straw.

"Spin this into gold by morning," he demanded, then left.

The girl wept at the impossible task. Suddenly, a strange little man appeared.

"Give me your necklace, and I will help you," he told her.

The girl handed it to him, and the strange little man sat in front of the spinning wheel and spun the straw into gold.

The next day, the delighted king took the miller's daughter to an even bigger room filled with straw.

"Spin this into gold, and you shall be my queen!" he said.

The strange little man appeared once more, but the girl had nothing left to give him.

"If you become queen," he told her, "you can give me your first-born child."

The girl agreed. Once again, he spun the straw into gold.

The next day, the king married the miller's daughter, and the new queen soon forgot all about the strange little man.

A year passed, and the queen had a bouncing baby boy. It did not take long for the little man to appear again.

"Please don't take my son," the queen begged.

"If you guess my name you can keep your baby—you have three days," said the little man.

For two nights after that the little man would appear in the baby's nursery. The queen would try to guess his name, but all of her guesses were wrong.

On the morning of the third day, one of the queen's servants was in the forest chopping logs when he saw a funny little man leaping around a fire and singing. He hid behind a tree and listened:

The queen will never win my game,
For Rumpelstiltskin is my name!

The servant hurried home to tell the queen.

That night, when the queen correctly guessed the little man's name, he was furious. He turned red with rage and ran off into the forest, never to be seen again.

Vintery, Mintery

Vintery, mintery, cutery, corn,
Apple seed and apple thorn;
Wire, briar, limber lock,
Three geese in a flock.
One flew east, and one flew west,
And one flew over the cuckoo's nest.

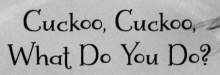

Cuckoo, Cuckoo,
What Do You Do?

Cuckoo, cuckoo, what do you do?
In April I open my bill;
In May I sing all day;
In June I change my tune;
In July away I fly;
In August away I must.

Three Ducks in a Brook

Look, look, look!
Three ducks in a brook.
One is white, and one is brown.
One is swimming upside down.
Look, look, look!
Three ducks in a brook.

Milly the Kangaroo

Milly was a kangaroo who loved to bounce and hop.
Every time she started—she didn't want to stop!
She bounced around all morning, and every afternoon.
She bounced around the forest, beside the blue lagoon.
"Look at me," she'd chuckle, bouncing to the sky.
"I'm a flying kangaroo, I can bounce so high!"
Milly never got fed up of bouncing up and down,
Even when she went to school or shopping in the town.
Her mom would hop beside her and offer things to eat,
But Milly never stopped at all—not even for a treat.
And when she snuggled down at night
Beneath the moonlight's beams …
She just kept right on hopping by bouncing in her dreams!

The Little Mermaid

Long ago, a mer-king lived under the sea with his six mermaid daughters, who all sang beautifully.

"When you are twenty-one," he said, "you can go to the surface and see the world above the sea."

One by one, the sisters visited the surface. At last, it was the turn of the youngest sister, and the little mermaid eagerly swam up to the ocean's surface.

On a nearby ship some people were throwing a party for the handsome prince on board.

As the little mermaid swam closer for a better look, a storm suddenly tossed the ship from side to side, and the prince was thrown into the churning water. The little mermaid dived down to rescue him.

Swimming close to the land, she gently pushed the unconscious prince onto the beach. His eyes flickered open, and he smiled before closing them again. As she swam away, the little mermaid saw some people coming down the beach to help him. So she dived beneath the waves and swam home.

The little mermaid told her sisters that she had fallen in love with the prince and longed to see him again.

"I know where his palace is," said her oldest sister. "I'll show you."

After that, the little mermaid swam to the surface every day, hoping to catch a glimpse of the prince.

"Can I become a human?" she asked her father one day.

"Only if a human falls in love with you," said the king gently.

But the little mermaid could not forget the prince. So she visited the sea witch.

"I can make a potion to make you human," hissed the witch. "But I will take your beautiful voice in return. You will only get it back if the prince falls in love with you."

The little mermaid loved the prince so much that she agreed. She swam to the prince's palace and drank the potion. She fell into a deep sleep. When she woke up, she was lying on the beach dressed in beautiful clothes. Where her shiny tail had been, she now had a pair of pale human legs. The little mermaid tried to stand, but her new legs wobbled and she stumbled.

As she fell, two strong arms reached out and caught her. The little mermaid looked up. It was the prince! She tried to speak, but her voice had gone, and she could only smile at her handsome rescuer.

The silent, beautiful stranger fascinated the prince. He grew very fond of her, and they spent their afternoons together.

One day, the prince told the little mermaid that he was getting married to a princess.

"My parents want me to do this," he sighed sadly. "But I love another girl. I don't know who she is, but she once rescued me from the sea."

The little mermaid was devastated, but without a voice, how could she tell the prince that she was that girl?

Just before the wedding, the prince walked with the little mermaid along the beach.

"Once I'm married, I won't be able to spend much time with you," he sighed.

The little mermaid nodded sadly. Suddenly, a huge wave crashed over the prince and the little mermaid, washing them out to sea. Without thinking, the little mermaid dived beneath the churning waves and grabbed the prince, taking him back to the shore.

"You're the girl who saved me before!" he cried.

The little mermaid smiled and nodded.

"I can't marry the princess. I love you," he sighed. "Will you marry me?" And as he kissed her, something magical happened. She could feel her voice returning!

"Yes!" she cried out with joy.

The happy couple were married the very next day. The little mermaid's dreams had come true, but she never forgot her family, or that she had once been a mermaid.

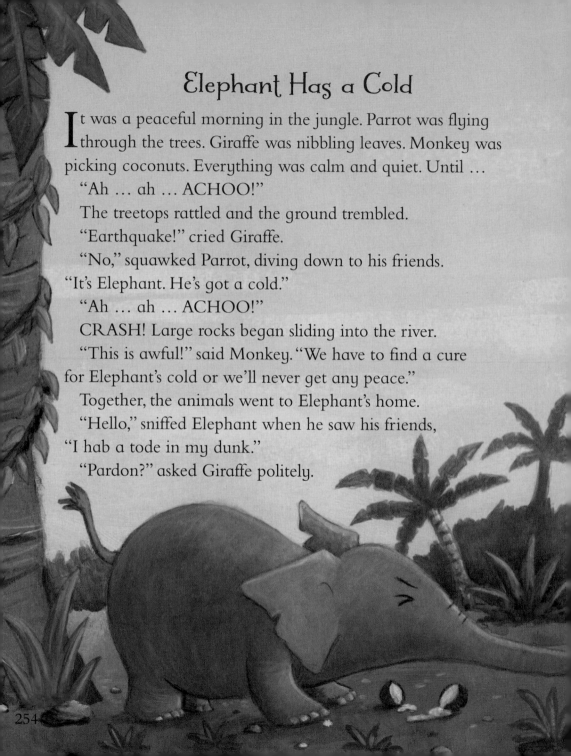

Elephant Has a Cold

It was a peaceful morning in the jungle. Parrot was flying through the trees. Giraffe was nibbling leaves. Monkey was picking coconuts. Everything was calm and quiet. Until …

"Ah … ah … ACHOO!"

The treetops rattled and the ground trembled.

"Earthquake!" cried Giraffe.

"No," squawked Parrot, diving down to his friends. "It's Elephant. He's got a cold."

"Ah … ah … ACHOO!"

CRASH! Large rocks began sliding into the river.

"This is awful!" said Monkey. "We have to find a cure for Elephant's cold or we'll never get any peace."

Together, the animals went to Elephant's home.

"Hello," sniffed Elephant when he saw his friends, "I hab a tode in my dunk."

"Pardon?" asked Giraffe politely.

"He says he has a cold in his trunk," Parrot explained.

"Warm coconut milk is very soothing," said Monkey. "Try this."

Elephant stuck out his trunk and tried to drink some of the milk.

"Slip-slurp … ah … ah … ACHOO!"

The sneeze sent the coconut milk splashing over everyone.

"Sorry," sniffed Elephant, miserably.

"We'll have to call Dr. Lion," said Parrot. "He's the only one who can cure Elephant's cold."

When Dr. Lion arrived in the jungle, he looked down Elephant's trunk.

"Say ah," he began. "Oh, yes. Just as I thought. The only cure for this cold is … lots of rest."

The animals gathered leaves and twigs to make a cozy bed for Elephant, and soon he was fast asleep.

Elephant slept for two whole days. On the third morning, Elephant woke up, stretched his trunk, and took a deep breath.

"Ah … ah … aaaaaaahhhh! I feel SO much better," he announced. "Thank you all for looking after me. You've been such good friends. And, of course, I would do the same for you!"

"That's good," sniffled Parrot, "because … ah … ah … ACHOO! I think I may be next."

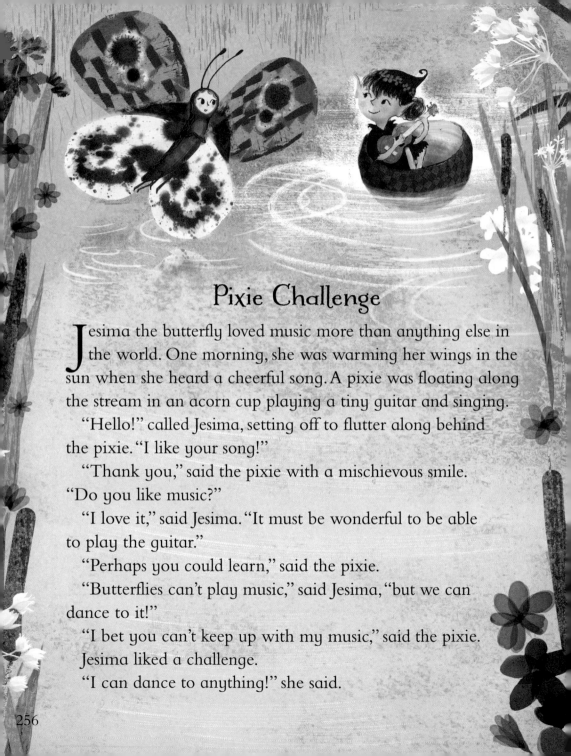

Pixie Challenge

Jesima the butterfly loved music more than anything else in the world. One morning, she was warming her wings in the sun when she heard a cheerful song. A pixie was floating along the stream in an acorn cup playing a tiny guitar and singing.

"Hello!" called Jesima, setting off to flutter along behind the pixie. "I like your song!"

"Thank you," said the pixie with a mischievous smile. "Do you like music?"

"I love it," said Jesima. "It must be wonderful to be able to play the guitar."

"Perhaps you could learn," said the pixie.

"Butterflies can't play music," said Jesima, "but we can dance to it!"

"I bet you can't keep up with my music," said the pixie.

Jesima liked a challenge.

"I can dance to anything!" she said.

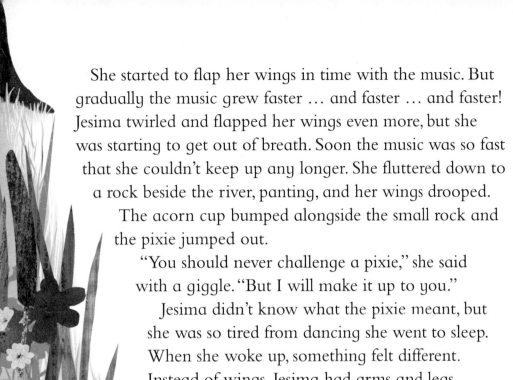

She started to flap her wings in time with the music. But gradually the music grew faster … and faster … and faster! Jesima twirled and flapped her wings even more, but she was starting to get out of breath. Soon the music was so fast that she couldn't keep up any longer. She fluttered down to a rock beside the river, panting, and her wings drooped.

The acorn cup bumped alongside the small rock and the pixie jumped out.

"You should never challenge a pixie," she said with a giggle. "But I will make it up to you."

Jesima didn't know what the pixie meant, but she was so tired from dancing she went to sleep. When she woke up, something felt different. Instead of wings, Jesima had arms and legs. She had been transformed into a pixie! Beside her, on the rock, lay a tiny guitar.

Jesima felt a playful giggle bubbling up inside her. She couldn't wait to start playing music—as well as a few mischievous pixie tricks of her own!

The Elves and the Shoemaker

There was once a poor shoemaker who lived with his wife. "We only have enough leather to make one more pair of shoes to sell," said the shoemaker.

So he cut out the leather, ready to stitch the next day, then went to bed.

That night, two elves crept into the shop, dressed in rags. They found the leather and set to work.

The next morning, the shoemaker was amazed to find the finest pair of shoes he had ever seen.

A rich gentleman saw the stylish shoes in the shop and tried them on. He was so delighted with the fit that he paid the shoemaker twice the asking price.

"We can buy more leather," the shoemaker told his wife.

That evening, the shoemaker cut out two more pairs of shoes from the leather, and went to bed.

During the night, the two elves crept into the shop again, and set to work on the leather.

In the morning, the shoemaker found two pairs of beautiful shoes. He sold them for more money than he had ever thought possible. Now the shoemaker had enough money to make four new pairs of shoes.

"Who is helping us?" asked the shoemaker's wife.

That night, the shoemaker cut out the new leather, then he and his wife hid and waited.

It wasn't long before the two little elves appeared and set to work on the leather.

"We must repay our little helpers for their kindness," the shoemaker told his wife.

"Let's make them some fine clothes," said his wife.

So they made the elves two little pairs of trousers, two smart coats, and two warm, woolly scarves.

That night, the shoemaker and his wife hid again and watched as the elves found their tiny outfits! They quickly dressed, then danced away happily into the night.

The shoemaker and his wife never saw the elves again. But they continued to make fine shoes and were never poor.

I Love My Grandma

Little Hedgehog and Grandma Hedgehog loved to play hide and seek together. One day, when Grandma went to find Little Hedgehog to help her make a picnic, he hid behind a bush.

"Where can Little Hedgehog be?" said Grandma.

Little Hedgehog giggled.

"Oh, well. I shall just have to make the picnic myself," said Grandma.

Little Hedgehog followed closely behind Grandma.

"I wish Little Hedgehog were here to help me pick juicy blackberries," said Grandma.

When she wasn't looking, Little Hedgehog picked the biggest blackberries he could reach and put them into Grandma's basket!

"What a lot of berries!" said Grandma, surprised. "I have enough for baking now."

Little Hedgehog scampered into Grandma's kitchen to find the best place to hide. He crouched down low so that Grandma couldn't see him.

"If only Little Hedgehog were here to help me," said Grandma.

Little Hedgehog licked his lips as Grandma Hedgehog poured sweet, scrumptious honey into her mixing bowl.

When Grandma wasn't looking, Little Hedgehog crept out from his hiding place to taste the honey. Then he quickly hid again.

"Someone has been tasting my honey," said Grandma. "And they have left sticky footprints!"

Grandma followed the teeny, tiny, sticky footprints across the kitchen and out into the garden.

"Someone has been playing hide and seek with me!" she said, smiling.

The sticky footprints went around and around the garden and stopped by the flowerpots.

"I've found you, Little Hedgehog!" cried Grandma.

But Little Hedgehog wasn't behind the flowerpots! He was … inside one!

"Surprise!" laughed Little Hedgehog.

"Well done, Little Hedgehog," said Grandma. "You're the best at hide and seek. I hope you're hungry, because our picnic is ready!"

"I am hungry," said Little Hedgehog, eagerly looking around the garden. "But where is the picnic?"

Grandma giggled. "You have to find it!" she said.

Little Hedgehog searched around the garden and soon found honey cookies and fruit salad.

Then Grandma brought out a giant blackberry cake.

"Yum! I love Grandma's picnics!" Little Hedgehog shouted happily. "And … I love my grandma!"

Jerry's Sandcastle

Jerry the hamster lived beside the sea. From his cage in the window, he watched children building sandcastles and splashing in the water.

"I wish I could play in the sand," he sighed.

Then, one night, Jerry reached through the bars and unlocked his cage. He slipped out and ran all the way to the beach.

"How wonderful!" he said, gazing at the moonlit sea.

As the waves crashed on the shore, he built turrets and battlements, dungeons and towers. He played in his sandcastle all night. Then he scurried into the sand dunes and fell fast asleep.

When Jerry woke up, the sea had washed his castle away. He looked up at his cage in the window. He missed the warm house and his cozy cage, and decided to go home. Of course, now he could visit the beach whenever he wanted!

"I can build sandcastles every night," he said. "And my next one will be even bigger!"

A Chilly Change

Edward the polar bear and his brother Charlie sold vanilla ice cream. But Edward had big ideas. He wanted to do something special with the ice cream—something different.

"Maybe I should make up some flavors," he said.

"Ice-cream flavors—that's crazy!" said Charlie. "No one will buy them. Vanilla is best, and I don't want to change."

"Change is exciting!" said Edward.

"Change is scary," said Charlie.

But Edward wouldn't give up. He thought about all the tastes he loved. Then he started inventing. Fish and iceberg flavor! Eel surprise! Salt and snowberries! Edward invented a new taste every day.

Edward and Charlie started to sell more and more ice cream. The news spread, and soon seals, gulls, and Arctic foxes were lining up to taste the incredible flavors.

"You were right," Charlie laughed at last. "I'm sorry. Sometimes, change is a very exciting thing indeed!"

Little Jack Horner

Little Jack Horner sat in the corner,
Eating his Christmas pie;
He put in his thumb, and pulled out a plum,
And said, "What a good boy am I!"

Betty Botter Bought Some Butter

Betty Botter bought some butter,
But she said, "The butter's bitter.
If I put it in my batter,
It will make my batter bitter.
But a bit of better butter
Will make my batter better."
So she bought some better butter.
Better than the bitter butter,
And she put it in her batter.
And her batter was not bitter.
So 'twas better Betty Botter
Bought a bit of better butter.

This rhyme is a tongue-twister.
Say it as quickly as you can.

Bread and Milk for Breakfast

Bread and milk for breakfast,
And woolen frocks to wear,
And a crumb for robin redbreast
On the cold days of the year.

Spin, Dame

Spin, Dame, spin
Your bread you must win;
Twist the thread and break it not,
Spin, Dame, spin.

Little Tommy Tucker

Little Tommy Tucker
Sings for his supper:
What shall we give him?
Brown bread and butter.
How shall he cut it
Without a knife?
How can he marry
Without a wife?

The Tortoise and the Hare

The tortoise and the hare were neighbors. Hare was always in a hurry, while Tortoise was happy to plod along, slowly and steadily.

One day, Tortoise was plodding along the road when Hare sped past him.

"You're so slow!" Hare called. "How do you ever get to where you're going?"

"I get everywhere I want to go!" Tortoise replied crossly. "I'll challenge you to a race."

"A race?" Hare laughed. "You don't stand a chance."

But they arranged a race for the next day, from an old oak tree all the way to the river, and asked Fox to judge it.

"On your marks … get set … go!" Fox shouted.

Hare sprinted ahead. Tortoise slowly set off.

After a few minutes, Hare could see the river ahead. He stopped. Tortoise was nowhere in sight.

"He won't be here for hours," he laughed. "I'll have a rest." Soon Hare dozed off.

Back along the path, Tortoise kept on, slow but steady.

After an hour, Hare woke up. He could just see Tortoise plodding toward him.

"He's so slow, he still won't be here for hours," Hare muttered, and went back to sleep.

When Hare woke up again, it was late afternoon. He looked down the road, but couldn't see Tortoise anywhere.

"I'll quickly finish the race, so I can go home," Hare sighed, bored with the race now.

Tortoise was waiting for him by the river.

"I've been here for hours!" cried Tortoise. "You are so slow!"

Hare tried to explain, but Tortoise and Fox wouldn't listen.

"But I'm faster!" Hare complained.

"The rules were simple," Fox said. "Tortoise won."

"The race was to get here first," Tortoise smiled, "not to run fastest. Slow and steady wins the race!"

Little Duck Has a Big Idea

Little Duck lived on a farm by a sparkling river. She loved exploring the riverbanks and talking to the rabbits, frogs, and field mice who lived there too.

In the summer, the river was a happy, crowded place. Little Duck especially loved to watch the arrival of the wild ducks. But now it was fall, and the wild ducks were getting ready to leave.

"Why are you going away?" she asked them.

"Nobody wants to stay here for the winter," replied the wild ducks. "It's too cold! We're flying south."

Little Duck had never been south. She loved her river home, but maybe it was time to try something new.

"I'm coming with you!" she shouted to the wild ducks, and swam off to tell her friends that she was leaving.

"Please don't go!" they cried. "Your home is here, with us."

But Little Duck wouldn't listen. Her mind was made up.

The next day, Little Duck followed some wild ducks high into the sky. But as she looked down at her friends and the winding river below, Little Duck began to feel sad.

"I don't want to leave my lovely river home and all my friends," she cried, swooping back down to the ground.

"I'm back," she called out.

"Who are you?" asked one of the rabbits.

"It's your friend, Little Duck!" replied Little Duck.

"Our friend flew off into the sky," squeaked a field mouse. "She's a wild duck now."

"No I'm not, I'm still Little Duck," Little Duck cried. "Don't you remember me?"

"Hmm," croaked a frog. "She looks like Little Duck. But Little Duck didn't want to stay here."

The animals burst into laughter.

"Stop that!" giggled Little Duck, realizing her friends were joking. "I belong here, with all of you."

"Welcome home, Little Duck!" said her friends. And Little Duck never flew away again.

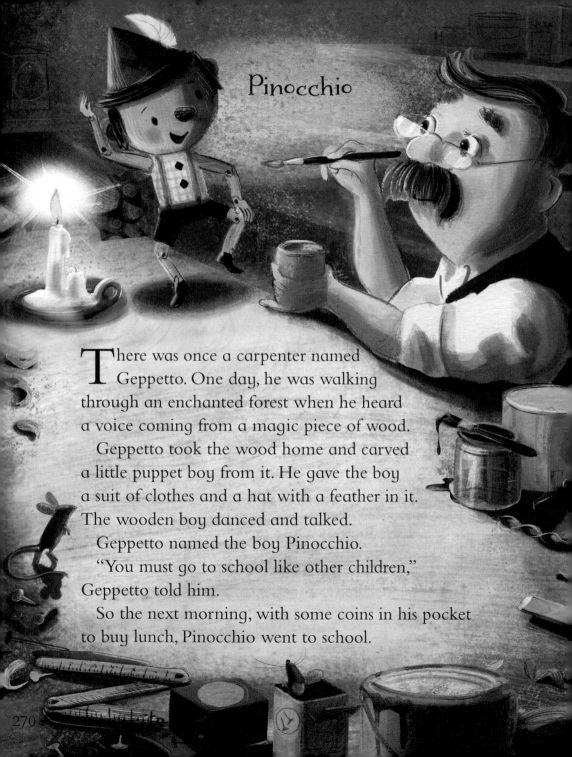

Pinocchio

There was once a carpenter named Geppetto. One day, he was walking through an enchanted forest when he heard a voice coming from a magic piece of wood.

Geppetto took the wood home and carved a little puppet boy from it. He gave the boy a suit of clothes and a hat with a feather in it. The wooden boy danced and talked.

Geppetto named the boy Pinocchio.

"You must go to school like other children," Geppetto told him.

So the next morning, with some coins in his pocket to buy lunch, Pinocchio went to school.

Along the way, a cricket hopped up onto his shoulder.

"You look like you could use a friend," he told Pinocchio. "I will help you learn right from wrong."

Further down the road, Pinocchio met a fox and a cat. They had heard his money jangling in his pocket.

"Come and play with us!" said the fox slyly.

"Pinocchio, you promised your father you would go to school," the cricket whispered.

But Pinocchio, not knowing any better, followed the cat and the fox into a dark forest.

"Plant your money here, and it will grow into a money tree," they told Pinocchio. "Just come back tomorrow, and you'll see."

The next morning, instead of going to school, Pinocchio went to find his money tree. But when he reached the spot where he'd buried his coins, there was no money tree, and his coins had gone.

"They played a trick on you," sighed his friend, the cricket. "They just wanted to get your money."

Pinocchio felt silly, but he pretended he didn't care, and stomped off into the forest. The little cricket begged him to go back to Geppetto, but Pinocchio wouldn't listen. Just as it was getting dark, they came to a tiny cottage. Pinocchio knocked on the door loudly, and a pretty fairy answered.

"We're lost," explained Pinocchio. "Please can you help us?"

The fairy invited them in and gave them some food.

"Why are you so far from home?" she asked kindly.

Pinocchio didn't want to tell her that he had disobeyed his father.

"I was chased by a giant!" he lied.

Suddenly, Pinocchio's nose grew a little.

"And I ran into the forest to escape!" he continued.

And Pinocchio's nose grew again!

"I have put a spell on you!" said the fairy. "Every time you tell a lie, your wooden nose will grow."

Pinocchio began to cry. "I won't tell any more lies," he promised.

The fairy waved her wand and Pinocchio's nose returned to normal.

"From now on I will do just as Father tells me," he said. But when he returned home, Geppetto wasn't there. He was out searching for Pinocchio!

"We must find Father and bring him home," he sobbed, feeling bad.

They began their search by the river. But when they got there, Pinocchio fell into the water. The cricket jumped in to help him, but an enormous fish swallowed them both.

There in the fish's tummy, they found Geppetto! He had been swallowed by the fish too.

Pinocchio hugged his father tightly. "I won't leave you again!" he said.

Then Pinocchio took the feather from his hat and tickled the fish.

"A ... a ... a ... choo!" The fish gave a mighty sneeze, and Geppetto, Pinocchio, and the cricket flew out of the fish's mouth, and landed on the riverbank.

That night, as Pinocchio slept in his own little bed, the kind fairy flew in through his window.

"You're a good, brave boy," she said, and she kissed him on the forehead.

When Pinocchio awoke the next morning, he found that he was no longer made from wood. He was a real boy! From then on he was always a good son to Geppetto, and the best of friends with the cricket, who didn't need to tell him right from wrong ever again.

A, B, C

A, B, C,
Our kitty's up the tree!
And now begins,
With a sneeze and a cough
To lick her long white stockings off.
No more she'll go into the snow.
Not she, not she, not she!

Little Wind

Little wind, blow on the hilltop;
Little wind, blow down the plain;
Little wind, blow up the sunshine,
Little wind, blow off the rain.

Twitching Whiskers

Twitching whiskers,
Big long ears,
Little bobtails
On their rears,
Still as statues,
One, two, three—
Then hippety hoppety,
You can't catch me!

The Wise Old Owl

There was an old owl who lived in an oak;
The more he heard, the less he spoke.
The less he spoke, the more he heard.
Why aren't we like that wise old bird?

In April

In April's sweet month,
When leaves start to spring,
Lambs skip like fairies,
And birds build and sing.

There Was an Old Crow

There was an old crow
Sat upon a clod:
There's an end of my song,
That's odd!

Chicken Little

One day, an acorn fell on Chicken Little's head, then rolled away.

"Oh, my," clucked Chicken Little, panicked. "THE SKY IS FALLING!"

"Cluck-a-cluck-cluck!" shrieked Henny Penny. "We must tell the king!"

So they flapped down the road, and met Cocky Locky.

"Where are you going in such a hurry?" he asked.

"THE SKY IS FALLING!" cried Chicken Little. "We're off to tell the king!"

"Cock-a-doodle-doo," crowed Cocky Locky. "I'll come, too!"

So Chicken Little, Henny Penny, and Cocky Locky rushed off to tell the king. Soon they met Ducky Lucky.

"Why are you flapping so?" she asked.

"THE SKY IS FALLING!" cried Chicken Little. "We're off to tell the king!"

"C-can I c-c-come?" quacked Ducky Lucky nervously.

So Chicken Little, Henny Penny, Cocky Locky, and Ducky Lucky rushed off to tell the king.

Soon they met Drakey Lakey.

"What's all this fuss?" he asked.

"THE SKY IS FALLING!" cried Chicken Little. "We're off to tell the king!"

"I'll join you," squawked Drakey Lakey.

So Chicken Little, Henny Penny, Cocky Locky, Ducky Lucky, and Drakey Lakey rushed off to tell the king.

Soon they met Goosey Loosey and Turkey Lurkey.

"What's ruffled your feathers?" Goosey Loosey asked.

"THE SKY IS FALLING!" cried Chicken Little. "We're off to tell the king!"

"Goodness," gobbled Turkey Lurkey.

"We'll come!" honked Goosey Loosey.

So Chicken Little, Henny Penny, Cocky Locky, Ducky Lucky, Drakey Lakey, Goosey Loosey, and Turkey Lurkey rushed off to tell the king.

Soon they met Foxy Loxy.

"Hello!" he said. "Where are you all going?"

"THE SKY IS FALLING!" cried Chicken Little. "We're off to tell the king!"

Foxy Loxy grinned slyly. "I know a short cut. Follow me."

So they did … right into Foxy Loxy's den!

"RUN!" cried Chicken Little.

And the seven birds ran home, flapping and flurrying, as fast as they could.

And they never did get to tell the king about the sky falling.

Hickety Pickety

Hickety Pickety, my black hen,
She lays eggs for gentlemen,
Sometimes nine, and sometimes ten,
Hickety Pickety, my black hen.

Cluck, Cluck, Cluck

Cluck, cluck, cluck, cluck, cluck,
Good morning, Mrs. Hen.
How many chickens have you got?
Madam, I've got ten.
Four of them are yellow,
And four of them are brown.
And two of them are speckled red,
The nicest in the town.

I Had a Little Hen

I had a little hen, the prettiest ever seen,
She washed up the dishes, and kept the house clean.
She went to the mill to fetch me some flour,
And always got home in less than an hour.
She baked me my bread, she brewed me my ale,
She sat by the fire and told a fine tale!

Can You Walk on Tiptoe?

Can you walk on tiptoe, as softly as a cat?
And can you slink along the road, softly, just like that?
Can you take enormous strides, like a great giraffe?
Or wibble-wobble-wibble, just like a new-born calf?

There Was a Crooked Man

There was a crooked man
And he walked a crooked mile,
He found a crooked sixpence
Upon a crooked stile.
He bought a crooked cat,
Which caught a crooked mouse,
And they all lived together
In a little crooked house.

279

Bunny Loves to Write

One lovely sunny day, Buster Bunny was going out to play in the park with his friends.

"Always carrying a book!" chuckled Mom. "What is it this time, Buster? An adventure? A ghost story?"

"It's not a storybook," smiled Buster. "It's a notebook. My teacher wants everyone in the class to make up a story."

"That sounds fun," said Mom. "What are you going to write?"

"I don't know," said Buster. "I can't think of anything!"

"Oh, you'll have lots of ideas soon," said Mom. "But write them down right away or you'll forget them!"

Buster set off to the park. Soon he met Francine the frog.

"Lend me a paw with this heavy picnic basket," she said.

"A picnic? It feels more like treasure!" grunted Buster.

Then he took out his notebook. "I've just had my first idea. My story could be about treasure!"

They kept walking toward the park, but soon Francine stopped.

"I'm sure I just saw Max," she said.

"Me too," said Buster, puzzled. "But it looks like he's disappeared."

"As if by magic!" smiled Francine.

"Magic, huh?" said Buster. "Maybe someone could do magic in my story. Like a wizard!"

Suddenly … BOO!

Max the mouse jumped out from a bush.

"Eek! You scared me!" laughed Francine.

"And you've given me another idea," said Buster. "Something scary. There could be spooky ghosts in my story!"

The three friends started crossing a stream near their friend Sam's house when … SPLASH! Buster slipped into the water.

"Phew!" grinned Buster. "At least my notebook didn't get wet! And I've just had another idea. One of the characters could live in the water."

"Like a mermaid," suggested Max.

"Hi, everyone," said Sam. "I'll be ready in a minute. Do you want to come up in the tree and wait?"

"What, up there?" gasped Francine. "No way! You're almost in the sky!"

"Now there's an idea," said Buster. "There could be planes in my story."

"Or space rockets," said Max.

"Or aliens!" said Francine.

When they got to the park, the friends met Bella, Buster's sister.

"Hi, everyone!" she said. "Hey, Buster, what are you writing?"

"I'm writing a story," said Buster. "I've had lots of ideas, and now I'm making them into a real adventure!"

"Cool," said Bella. "Can we hear it?"

"Okay ..." said Buster. "But it isn't finished yet."

Buster opened his notebook and began to read. "Once upon a time, there were a brother and a sister named Gus and Ella ..."

"That's you and me!" giggled Bella.

"They lived in a town next to a friendly wizard," continued Buster. "He let the children play in his haunted castle."

"A wizard! I love stories about magic!" cried Francine.

"Ooh, ghosts! Great!" said Max.

"One day, Gus and Ella found a chest in the attic. They opened the lid. The chest was full of gold!" read Buster. "They had found the lost treasure of Meowlin! But the very next night, the treasure vanished. Where had it gone?"

Buster turned the page and continued, "In the castle moat lived a frog named Fiona, who said aliens from Mars had stolen the treasure! So the wizard waved his wand, and they all flew to Mars by magic!"

Buster stopped reading and sighed, "That's as far as I got."

"We'll help you finish it!" cried Sam.

Everyone took turns writing in Buster's notebook.

"Okay," he said when they were finished. "Here's the rest of the story! I'll read it to you."

"The wizard tricked the
aliens and took back the chest. Everyone
sneaked into a rocket and escaped. But the aliens followed
them and caught them! Then a ghost scared the aliens away
for good!" Buster said as he finished the story.

"Hooray!" everyone cheered.

"There's just one last thing to add,"
continued Buster. And he wrote:

"They all lived happily ever after. THE END."

The Fuzzy Caterpillar

The fuzzy caterpillar
Curled up on a leaf,
Spun her little chrysalis
And then fell fast asleep.
While she was a-sleeping
She dreamed that she could fly,
And later when she woke up
She was a butterfly!

Cobweb Races

No wonder spiders wear bare feet
To run their cobweb races.
Suppose they had to have eight shoes,
How would they tie their laces?

The Snail

The snail he lives in his hard round house,
In the orchard, under the tree:
Says he, "I have but a single room;
But it's large enough for me."

Flying High, Swooping Low

Flying high, swooping low,
Loop-the-loop and around they go.
Catching currents, soaring fast,
Feathered friends come sweeping past.

The Pigeon

A pigeon and a pigeon's son
Once went to town to buy a bun.
They couldn't decide on a plum or plain,
And so they flew back home again.

What Does the Donkey Say?

What does the donkey say?
Hee-haw, hee-haw.
What does the blackbird say?
Caw, caw, caw.
What does the cat say?
Meow, meow, meow.
What does the dog say?
Bow-wow, bow-wow.

Blossom the Cow

Blossom the cow lived on a big farm at the top of a hill. Sometimes visitors came to stay at the farm for a vacation. Mrs. Pinstripe, the farmer's wife, looked after the guests while her husband, the farmer, looked after the animals.

One Monday morning, Mrs. Pinstripe noticed that none of her guests had eaten their breakfast.

"Is anything wrong?" Mrs. Pinstripe asked them.

"Erm, well, the butter and milk taste funny," said one guest.

"And the yogurt," said another.

"How odd! Yesterday's milk was fine," Mrs. Pinstripe told her husband. "It must be Blossom."

But Blossom had always won prizes for her milk as it was so tasty. What could be wrong?

All that day, and for the rest of the week, the farmer watched Blossom eat grass. Every evening, after milking her, he tasted the milk. It was lovely and sweet.

On Sunday, Blossom seemed very excited. As soon as the farmer let her into the field, she went straight to the stream and waited.

Soon, a group of children walked into the field and laid a large rug on the grass next to Blossom. Then they started to eat from their picnic basket. Every time they offered Blossom something, she turned her head away, until she saw … CHIPS! Onion-flavored, spicy-barbecue-flavored, salt-and-vinegar-flavored—any flavor with a strong taste!

The farmer was amazed. "So that's why her milk tastes strange!" he said.

The next Sunday evening, after another picnic with the children, the farmer gave Blossom a handful of extra-strong peppermints. Then, he waited a while for the minty flavor to go into her milk.

On Monday morning, Mrs. Pinstripe watched as her guests ate and drank everything. Then they asked for more!

"Mrs. Pinstripe," said one of the guests, "this peppermint-flavored yogurt is delicious."

Mrs. Pinstripe smiled at her husband and whispered, "If only they knew."

287

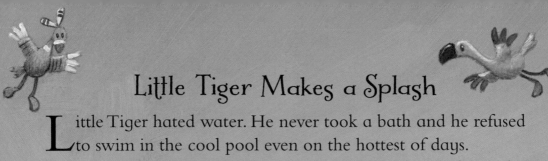

Little Tiger Makes a Splash

Little Tiger hated water. He never took a bath and he refused to swim in the cool pool even on the hottest of days.

"You're filthy and your fur is smelly! You need a wash," said Mommy Tiger one day.

"I like being muddy and tangled," Little Tiger replied, and slouched off to laze on a tree branch that hung over the pool.

The air was filled with the soothing sounds of birds twittering and his family splashing in the pool below.

Before long, Little Tiger had drifted off to sleep. He dreamed that he was not a tiger, but a bird twittering in a tree. He spread his feathery wings and leaped into the air … SPLOSH!

Little Tiger suddenly found himself in the water. He was about to scramble to the bank, when he realized how wonderfully cool he felt. And how much fun it was to splash!

Now Little Tiger loves swimming in the pool every day— and he is very clean, too!

Where's Barney?

Mia Meerkat always went to sleep with her teddy, Barney, but one bedtime Barney could not be found.

"We have to find him or none of us will sleep, especially Mia," said Mama.

Mama and Papa searched in the sand dunes and hunted in tunnels. They burrowed and rummaged and scoured.

Then Mama spotted Barney—in the paws of a sleeping jackal!

"Uh-oh," she gulped. "This could be tricky."

She pulled Barney free, but then the jackal opened his eyes.

"I found that teddy!" he wailed.

Mama threw Barney to Papa, and the jackal bounded after him. Papa threw Barney back to Mama, and the jackal chased her. Just in the nick of time, they reached their underground home, and the jackal skulked off. Panting, Mama went into Mia's bedroom. But Mia wasn't waiting for Barney … she was fast asleep!

In the morning, Mia got a big surprise. Mama and Papa were snoring on her bedroom floor—cuddling Barney!

The Boy Who Cried Wolf

Once there was a boy named Peter who lived in a little village in the mountains with his parents, who were sheep farmers. It was Peter's job to watch over the flock and protect the sheep from wolves.

Every day, Peter sat on the mountainside watching the flock. It was very quiet with no one but sheep for company. No wolves ever came to eat the sheep.

"Oh, I wish something exciting would happen," groaned Peter. "I'm so bored!"

Finally, one day, Peter couldn't stand it any more. He started shouting at the top of his voice:

"WOLF! HELP! WOLF!"

Down in the village, a man heard Peter's cries.

"Quick!" he shouted. "There's a wolf attacking the sheep."

The villagers grabbed their axes, forks, and shovels and ran up the mountain to where Peter was shepherding his flock.

When they got there, the sheep were grazing peacefully.

"Where's the wolf?" one of the villagers cried.

Peter roared with laughter. "There's no wolf. I was just playing!"

The villagers were very angry. "You mustn't cry wolf when there isn't one," they said.

That night Peter got a telling-off from his mother and was sent to bed without any supper.

For a while after this, Peter managed to behave himself, and the villagers soon forgot about his trick.

Then one day, Peter was bored again. Laughing, he picked up some sticks and started banging them hard together. Then at the top of his voice, he shouted, "WOLF! Help! WOLF! There's a big wolf eating the sheep!"

Down in the village, a crowd of people started gathering when they heard the loud banging and shouting.

"It's Peter," someone cried. "Quick, there must be a wolf on the prowl."

Once again, the villagers grabbed their axes, forks, and shovels. They ran up the mountain to chase away the wolf and save poor Peter and his sheep.

And once again, when they got there,
the sheep were grazing peacefully.

"Peter, what's happened?" shouted
one man angrily.

"There's no wolf," laughed Peter.
"I was only playing."

"You shouldn't do that," said another man. "It's not
good to lie."

That night, Peter got an even bigger telling-off from
his mother, and once again had to go to bed without
any supper.

Peter decided that he would really try and behave
himself from now on, and soon the incident was forgotten.

A few weeks later, while Peter stood counting
the sheep to pass the time, he noticed that some
of them were bleating nervously.

He climbed up a tree to see what
was upsetting them.

To his horror, he saw a big wolf creeping through the grass toward the flock.

Shaking with fear, he started screaming, "WOLF! Help! WOLF! Please hurry, there's a big wolf about to eat the sheep!"

A few people down in the village heard his cries for help, but they kept on with their business as usual.

"It's only Peter playing another trick," they said to each other. "Does he think he can fool us again?"

And so nobody went to Peter's rescue.

By nightfall, when Peter hadn't returned, his parents became concerned. Peter never missed his supper—something bad must have happened.

The villagers hurried up the mountain, carrying flaming torches to light their way.

A terrible sight met their eyes. All the sheep were gone! There really had been a wolf this time.

Peter was still in the tree, shaking and crying.

"I cried out wolf! Why didn't you come?" he wept.

"Nobody believes a liar, even when he's speaking the truth," said Peter's father, helping him climb out of the tree. Peter hung on to his father all the way home. He never wanted to see another wolf ever again.

And Peter finally really learned his lesson. He never told a lie again, and he always got to eat his dinner.

I Love You When

I love you when it's warm and sunny.
I love you when you're being funny.
I love you when it's wet outside.
I love you when I want to hide.

I love you when it's very breezy!
I even love you when you're sneezy.
I love you when we rush to and fro,
and I love you when there's nowhere to go.

I love you when you're feeling sleepy.
I love you when you're sad and weepy.
I love you when you giggle …
when you wiggle …
when you wriggle …

I love you when you're snuggly.
I love you when you're huggly.
I love you when you say, "I love you too."
But mostly I love you whenever I'm with you.

Little Red Riding Hood

There was once a sweet little girl who always wore a lovely red cape with a hood. So everyone called her Little Red Riding Hood.

"Granny isn't feeling well," said her mother one morning. "Take her this basket of food, and don't talk to any strangers!"

So Little Red Riding Hood took the basket and set off right away.

Very soon she met a wolf.

"Hello," said the wolf. "Where are you going?"

"I'm visiting my sick granny," replied Little Red Riding Hood, forgetting her mother's warning. "She lives on the other side of these woods."

While Little Red Riding Hood picked some flowers for Granny, the wolf raced down the path to the old lady's cottage.

He opened the door, and before Granny had a chance to shout for help, the wicked creature opened his huge jaws and swallowed her whole! Then he climbed into her bed, pulled the covers up under his chin and waited.

Soon, Little Red Riding Hood reached Granny's house with her basket of food and bunch of flowers.

When she went into the bedroom, she gasped in surprise. Her granny didn't look well at all!

"Granny," she exclaimed. "Your ears are enormous!"

"All the better to hear you with," growled the wolf.

"And your eyes are as big as saucers," she gulped.

"All the better to see you with," snarled the wolf.

"And your teeth are so … pointed!" she gasped.

"All the better to EAT you with!" roared the wolf, and he swallowed Little Red Riding Hood in one GULP! Then he fell fast asleep.

Luckily, a nearby woodcutter heard some loud snoring sounds coming from the cottage.

He tiptoed inside and found the sleeping wolf … with his tummy bulging.

So he tipped the wolf upside-down and shook him hard. Out fell Little Red Riding Hood, and out fell Granny!

Granny was so furious, she chased the wolf far into the woods and they never saw him again!

Flamingo's Dance Class

Flamingo was a very elegant bird. She never tripped over or bumped into things. But the other animals in the jungle weren't always so graceful.

"Look out!" Flamingo exclaimed as Elephant barged into a tree.

"Be careful!" she cried when Hippo wiped mud on her feathers.

"Watch your step!" she squeaked as Crocodile trampled over her toes. "You're all so clumsy!"

Elephant, Hippo, and Crocodile felt embarrassed. They didn't want the other animals to think they were clumsy.

"A ballet lesson will help," said Flamingo.

First, she showed her class how to do a pirouette.

"Now it's your turn," she said.

Elephant did her best, but she was so heavy that she just drilled a hole deep into the ground and got her leg stuck.

"Perhaps a pirouette is too hard," said Flamingo. "Try this instead."

She stood on one leg in a beautiful pose, and tucked the other leg under her body. Hippo tried to copy her, but he accidentally kicked a tree and knocked it down. Flamingo groaned.

"Perhaps you would be more graceful if you looked prettier," she said, handing them some tutus. "Try these on."

But poor Crocodile's belly was so low to the ground that his tutu dragged in the mud.

"I don't think we'll ever be as elegant as you, Flamingo," said Elephant sadly.

Flamingo sighed and looked at her friends. Elephant could use her trunk to pick leaves and berries gently. Hippo dived underwater without bumping into anything, and when Crocodile glided into the swamp he didn't make a single ripple.

Suddenly, Flamingo felt very silly. Why was she trying to change her friends? When they acted naturally, they all looked graceful.

"I'm sorry I called you clumsy," she said. "You're perfect just the way you are!"

I Love My Grandpa

One sunny afternoon, Little Bear went for a walk by the river with Grandpa Bear.

"Shall we wade in the water, Little Bear?"

Little Bear shook his head. "I don't like water, Grandpa," he said.

"Let's just put one paw in," said Grandpa, "and see what it feels like."

Grandpa Bear put one paw in the water.

"Ah!" he said. "That feels good!"

Little Bear put only the tip of his paw in. Then he giggled.

"The water tickles!" he said, and he put the rest of his paw in and waved it about. "Wheeee!"

Grandpa Bear put two paws in. So did Little Bear.

Then Little Bear put all four of his little paws into the cool water.

"Well done, Little Bear!" said Grandpa. "You're wading! Now, are you ready to make a splash?"

Little Bear kicked his feet, making splashes with a swoosh-swoosh-swoosh! Then suddenly …

SPLOOSH!

In jumped Grandpa Bear, making a gigantic splash!

"Yippee!" cried Little Bear.

"Shall we have a swim now, Little Bear?" said Grandpa Bear.

Little Bear shook his head. "I can't swim, Grandpa!" he said.

"Let's just float," said Grandpa, "and see what it feels like. I will hold you."

When Little Bear felt his grandpa holding him,
he lifted up one paw at a time, until …

"You're floating!" said Grandpa Bear. "Now, how
about some more splashing?"

Little Bear kicked his feet, making more swoosh-swooshes!
And suddenly …

"You're swimming, Little Bear!" said Grandpa.

Little Bear swam around and around his grandpa.

"You're the best little swimmer there is," said Grandpa
Bear proudly.

When it was time to get out, Grandpa Bear helped Little
Bear climb out of the water. Then they both wriggled and
jiggled to get dry, spraying water all about.

Grandpa Bear gave Little Bear a warming hug.

"Do you like water now, Little Bear?" he asked, smiling.

Little Bear grinned. "I love water!" he shouted happily.
"And … I love my grandpa!"

The Sick Day

Rabbit didn't feel well, so his mother wrapped him up in a fluffy blanket and called Dr. Hare.

"Maybe he's got a fever," said Dr. Hare. "Cool him down with carrot salad."

Rabbit's mother made some carrot salad, but Rabbit wasn't hungry.

"Maybe he's got a cold," said Dr. Hare. "Warm him up with carrot soup."

Rabbit's mother cooked up a delicious soup, but Rabbit couldn't even eat a spoonful.

"What do you want, Rabbit?" asked Dr. Hare kindly. Rabbit pointed at his mother, who stroked his soft fur and kissed his pink nose. She gave him a big, rabbity cuddle.

"I'm feeling better already," said Rabbit happily.

His mother made him giggle with some funny stories. By bedtime, Rabbit felt well again. His father came home, and Rabbit told him all about the doctor.

"I didn't need salad or soup," he said. "I needed cuddles and funny stories!"

"They're the best medicine of all," said his father wisely.

Oak Tree Hospital

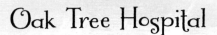

One day, Mrs. Mouse arrived at Oak Tree Hospital in a fluster. "Please help!" she cried. "My son Luca has a thimble stuck on his head!"

The squirrel nurse tried to pull the thimble off, but Luca yelled, "Ouch!" and "Stop!" so she did. The squirrel doctor smeared Luca's head with honey. It made him very sticky and got in his eyes and ears, but it didn't move the thimble one bit. Then the squirrel nurse had a thought.

"Luca, can you waggle your ears and wiggle your eyebrows?" she asked.

Luca waggled and wiggled as hard as he could, while the squirrel nurse and Mrs. Mouse and the squirrel doctor tugged on the thimble. And with a loud POP! the thimble flew into the air and hit the squirrel doctor on the nose.

From then on, just in case, Mrs. Mouse made Luca practice waggling and wiggling every single day—and kept him well away from thimbles!

Five Currant Buns

Five currant buns in the baker's shop,
Big and round with a cherry on the top.

Along came *(insert name)* with a penny one day,
Bought a currant bun and took it away.
Four currant buns in the baker's shop,
Big and round with a cherry on the top.

Along came *(insert name)* with a penny one day,
Bought a currant bun and took it away.
(Repeat the rhyme, counting down from
three currant buns to no currant buns …)

No currant buns in the baker's shop,
Nothing big and round with a cherry on the top.
Along came *(insert name)* with a penny one day,
"Sorry," said the baker,
"No more currant buns today."

Hot Cross Buns

Hot cross buns!
Hot cross buns!
One a penny, two a penny,
Hot cross buns!
If you have no daughters,
Give them to your sons.
One a penny, two a penny,
Hot cross buns!

Sing a Song of Sixpence

Sing a song of sixpence
A pocket full of rye.
Four and twenty blackbirds
Baked in a pie.
When the pie was opened
The birds began to sing.
Now wasn't that a dainty dish
To set before the king?

From Wibbleton to Wobbleton

From Wibbleton to Wobbleton
is fifteen miles,
From Wobbleton to Wibbleton
is fifteen miles,
From Wibbleton to Wobbleton,
From Wobbleton to Wibbleton,
From Wibbleton to Wobbleton
is fifteen miles.

Hark! Hark!

Hark! Hark!
The dogs do bark,
Beggars are coming to town:
Some in rags,
Some in tags,
And some in velvet gowns.

Handy Spandy

Handy Spandy, Jack-a-dandy
Loved plum cake and sugar candy;
He bought some at a grocer's shop,
And out he came, hop, hop, hop.

Seesaw, Sacradown

Seesaw, Sacradown,
Which is the way to London Town?
One foot up and one foot down,
That's the way to London Town.

The House That Jack Built

This is the house that Jack built.
This is the man all tattered and torn,
That kissed the maiden all forlorn,
That milked the cow with the crumpled horn,
That tossed the dog,
That worried the cat,
That killed the rat,
That ate the malt
That lay in the house that Jack built.

If Wishes Were Horses

If wishes were horses,
Beggars would ride;
If turnips were watches,
I'd wear one by my side.

Very Best Friends

When Grace moved into her new house, she loved her pretty new bedroom and the garden full of trees. But she missed all her friends.

Grace's favorite game was dressing up, but it was no fun to play on her own.

One day, Grace was fluttering around the garden in her favorite fairy dress and sparkling wings, when she heard a girl's voice in the yard next door. She looked over the fence, but all she could see were black clothes and long, tangled hair.

"Oh dear," Grace said. "I like to wear pretty colors and have neat hair! I don't think we'll ever be friends."

A few days later, Grace saw the girl from next door again. But this time she was wearing a pretty dress and purple shoes. Then Grace noticed that the girl was crying.

"Hello," Grace said softly. "Why are you crying?"

The girl told Grace her name was Emma, and then sighed: "I was flying around in my bumblebee costume, and the wings caught on a tree and ripped!"

"Do you like dressing up?" asked Grace.

Emma nodded. "It's my favorite game!"

"It's mine too!" said Grace excitedly. "You can borrow my fairy wings, if you like!"

"Thank you!" said Emma happily.

Grace and Emma spent all afternoon dressing up.

Next day, Emma knocked on Grace's door. She was wearing a fairy godmother costume.

"Thank you for letting me use your fairy wings," she said.

"Thank you for playing with me!" said Grace.

"I've come to grant you a wish," said Emma.

"I wish …" said Grace, "that we will always be best friends."

Emma waved her magic wand … and, smiling, took her new friend's hand in hers, and gave it a squeeze.

"Let's be the very best friends ever!" said Emma.

"This is a real wish come true!" sighed Grace. And the two girls did a happy, twirly fairy dance together.

I'll Have to Think Again

Frog was sitting on a lily pad, reading a cookbook. It was his birthday, and he wanted to make a birthday cake to surprise his friends. He wrote a list of the ingredients, and set out to get them.

First Frog went to his friend, the miller, to get a bag of flour.

"How will you get the flour home?" asked the miller.

"I'll swim up the river with it," replied Frog.

"But the flour will get wet," warned the miller, "and it will be no use to you at all."

"Oh," said Frog. "I'll have to think again."

Next, Frog went to see his friend, Brown Cow, for a bucket of her milk.

"How will you get the milk home without spilling it into the river?" asked Brown Cow.

"Oh, I don't really know," mumbled Frog. "I'll have to think again."

Frog decided to visit Speckled Hen for some eggs.

"Take as many as you need," she told Frog, "but how will you get them home?"

"I'll tuck the eggs under my chin," said Frog, happily.

"But you might drop them and then they'll break," replied Speckled Hen.

"Oh," croaked Frog, and a tear fell from the corner of his eye. "I'll just have to think again."

Frog returned to his lily pad, empty-handed and miserable. The sun was warm and he was tired, so he drifted off to sleep.

"Happy birthday to you …"

Suddenly, Frog woke up. On the bank of the pond stood all his friends, singing. The miller was holding a birthday cake.

"But … how?" gasped Frog.

"We wanted to surprise you," said the miller. "Brown Cow provided the milk, Speckled Hen laid some eggs, and I mixed the ingredients with my flour and baked you a cake."

"Wow! Thank you," grinned Frog. "But I was going to make a cake to surprise you."

"Well," his friends laughed, "you'll have to think again!"

I Plant a Little Seed

I plant a little seed in the cold, cold ground,
Out comes the yellow sun, big and round,
Down come the raindrops, soft and slow,
Up comes the flower, grow, grow, grow.

One Man Went to Mow

One man went to mow,
Went to mow a meadow,
One man and his dog,
Went to mow a meadow.
Two men went to mow,
Went to mow a meadow,
Two men, one man, and his dog,
Went to mow a meadow.

*You can keep adding verses
as far as you can count.*

A Swarm of Bees in May

A swarm of bees in May is worth a load of hay;
A swarm of bees in June is worth a silver spoon;
A swarm of bees in July is not worth a fly.

Four Seeds in a Row

Four seeds in a row,
Four seeds in a row.
One for the mouse,
One for the crow,
One to rot and one to grow.

Grinding Corn

Early in the misty morn,
The miller's up to grind some corn.
Wheels turn, sacks will fill,
As he grinds corn in his mill.

Jade's First Race

It was Jade the green car's first-ever race. She was very excited and she couldn't stop grinning.

"I hope I get a medal!" she cried.

But around the first bend in the track, she saw Ruby the red car with a flat tire. So Jade stopped to replace it.

Around the next bend, Yasmin the yellow car called for help.

"Need water!" she panted. So Jade gave her some water. Around the next bend, she saw Ben the blue car.

"I've run out of gas!" Ben spluttered.

Jade lent him some gas, and Ben zoomed off.

But after helping all the other cars, Jade finished the race in last place.

"I'll never get a medal now," she sighed, dipping her headlights as the other cars gathered around.

"Jade was last because she stopped to help us," said Ruby.

"She's the real winner," said Yasmin.

"Jade deserves a medal," said Ben. "Three cheers for the kindest car in the race!"

Brown Bear's Bus Ride

Every day a shiny blue bus full of people roared past Brown Bear's home.

"I wish I could ride on the bus," he murmured. "I wonder where it goes."

Then one morning, a bus ticket fluttered onto the grass outside his cave. He picked it up with trembling paws. His dream had come true!

When Brown Bear climbed onto the bus, the driver stalled the engine in shock and the passengers squealed. Brown Bear couldn't understand why everyone looked so scared. But one little girl wasn't afraid.

"Hello," she smiled, slipping her hand into his paw. "I'm Ella."

When the other passengers saw how brave Ella was, they felt silly. They all shook hands with Brown Bear as the bus set off past the farm, through the town, and over the bridges. Now he knew where the bus went!

At the end of his ride, Ella kissed him and the passengers hugged him goodbye.

"Come back soon," they said. "This bus is now bear-friendly!"

Unicorn Magic

Once upon a time there were two little unicorns named Lottie and Lulu, and they lived with their mother in a cave on top of a mountain.

Unicorns are magical creatures, and their twisty horns are full of spells and enchantments. But little unicorns have to learn how to use their magic … and they don't always get it right!

One day, Lottie and Lulu's mother went to visit some friends. As soon as she had trotted out of sight, Lottie and Lulu shared a big smile.

"Let's give her a surprise," said Lottie. "Let's magically tidy up the cave."

Lottie said the first spell, and purple sparkles flew out of her twisty horn and hit a messy heap of hay in the corner. But instead of tidying it up, the spell turned the hay purple.

"Let me try," said Lulu. As she said her spell, green sparkles zipped out of her twisty horn and hit a bowl of apples. They turned into beetles and scuttled off.

"Let's do the dusting," said Lottie. She tried to make the dust vanish, but it turned into a cloud of glitter instead.

"Oh, no! What a mess," gasped Lulu.

Things got worse and worse. Every spell that Lottie and Lulu tried went wrong. They made their beds with honey instead of heather. They covered the ceiling with blue cornflowers. They turned the ribbons that their mother decorated her mane with into butterflies.

And that was when their mother came back.

"Oh, dear," she said, looking around at the chaos.

"We're sorry," said Lulu. "We were trying to help, but every spell went wrong."

Their mother nuzzled them both.

"It's all right," she said. "It is a bit messy, but I don't think I have ever seen the cave looking so pretty and colorful!"

There Was an Old Woman
Who Lived in a Shoe

There was an old woman who lived in a shoe,
She had so many children she didn't know what to do;
She gave them some broth without any bread;
And scolded them soundly and put them to bed.

There Was an Old Woman
and Nothing She Had

There was an old woman
And nothing she had,
And so this old woman
Was said to be sad.
She'd nothing to ask,
And nothing to give,
And when she did die
She'd nothing to leave.

There Was an Old Woman
and What Do You Think?

There was an old woman, and what do you think?
She lived upon nothing but victuals and drink:
Victuals and drink were the chief of her diet;
This tiresome old woman could never be quiet.

There Was an Old Woman
Went Up in a Basket

There was an old woman went up in a basket,
Seventy times as high as the moon;
What she did there I could not but ask it,
For in her hand she carried a broom.
"Old woman, old woman, old woman," said I,
"Whither, oh whither, oh whither so high?"
"To sweep the cobwebs from the sky,
And I shall be back again, by and by."

There Was an Old Woman
Lived Under the Hill

There was an old woman
Lived under the hill,
And if she's not gone
She lives there still.

There Was an Old Woman
Called Nothing-at-all

There was an old woman called Nothing-at-all,
Who rejoiced in a dwelling exceedingly small;
A man stretched his mouth to its utmost extent,
And down at one gulp house and old woman went.

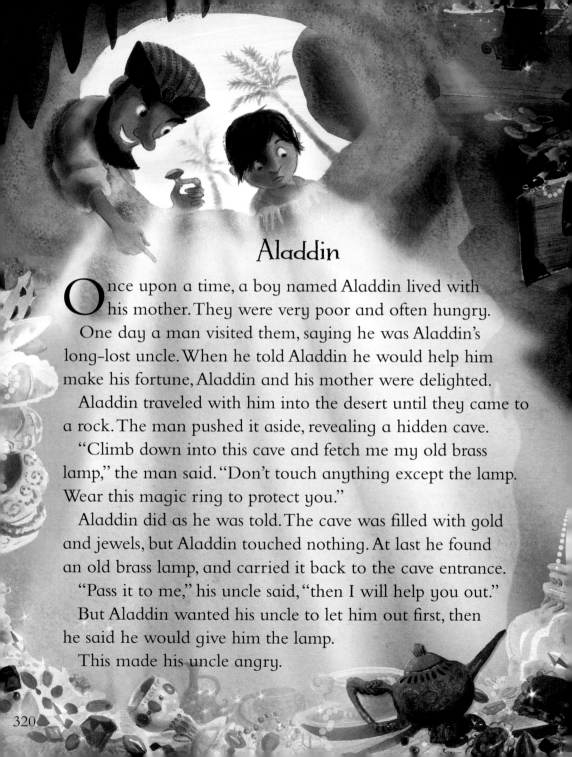

Aladdin

Once upon a time, a boy named Aladdin lived with his mother. They were very poor and often hungry.

One day a man visited them, saying he was Aladdin's long-lost uncle. When he told Aladdin he would help him make his fortune, Aladdin and his mother were delighted.

Aladdin traveled with him into the desert until they came to a rock. The man pushed it aside, revealing a hidden cave.

"Climb down into this cave and fetch me my old brass lamp," the man said. "Don't touch anything except the lamp. Wear this magic ring to protect you."

Aladdin did as he was told. The cave was filled with gold and jewels, but Aladdin touched nothing. At last he found an old brass lamp, and carried it back to the cave entrance.

"Pass it to me," his uncle said, "then I will help you out."

But Aladdin wanted his uncle to let him out first, then he said he would give him the lamp.

This made his uncle angry.

"Fool!" the man roared, and he rolled the rock back over the cave, trapping Aladdin inside.

"Uncle!" Aladdin cried. "Let me out!"

"I'm not your uncle," said the man. "I'm a sorcerer! Stay there for good if you won't give me the lamp."

As Aladdin wrung his hands in despair, he rubbed the magic ring on his finger.

Suddenly, a genie sprang out and asked: "What do you require, master?"

Astonished, Aladdin told the genie to take him home. In a flash, Aladdin was outside his mother's house.

Still poor and hungry, Aladdin polished the old lamp, hoping to sell it to get money for food. But as he rubbed the lamp clean, another genie jumped out.

This time, Aladdin asked for food and money so that he and his mother could live in comfort.

Life went on happily until, one day, Aladdin fell hopelessly in love with the emperor's beautiful daughter. But how could he, Aladdin, marry a princess? Suddenly, he had an idea … he asked the genie of the lamp for gifts to give to the princess.

When the princess thanked Aladdin for the gifts, she fell in love with him. They were soon married, and Aladdin asked the genie to build them a beautiful palace.

Hearing that a wealthy stranger had married the princess, the wicked sorcerer guessed that Aladdin must have escaped with the lamp.

One day, when Aladdin was out, the sorcerer disguised himself as a poor tradesman. He stood outside the palace calling out, "New lamps for old! New lamps for old!"

Aladdin's wife gave her husband's old brass lamp to the sorcerer, who snatched it away and rubbed the lamp. He commanded the genie to carry the palace and the princess far away.

"Oh, no!" cried Aladdin, when he discovered his wife and home gone.

Quickly, he rubbed the magic ring to make the genie appear.

"Please bring back my wife and palace!" Aladdin pleaded.

"Sorry, master, I can't!" said the genie. "I am less powerful than the genie of the lamp."

"Then take me to her and I'll win her back!" Aladdin cried.

At once, he found himself in a strange city, but outside his own palace. Through a window he saw his wife crying, and the sorcerer sleeping. Aladdin crept into the palace. He grabbed the magic lamp and rubbed it.

"What do you require, master?" asked the genie.

"Take us right back home," Aladdin said, "and shut this wicked sorcerer in the cave for a thousand years!"

In a moment, the palace was back where it belonged. With the sorcerer gone, Aladdin and the princess were safe, and they never needed to call on the genie again.

Down With the Lambs

Down with the lambs,
Up with the lark,
Run to bed, children,
Before it gets dark.

Brown Bird

Little brown bird,
Where do you live?
"Up in yonder wood, sir,
On a hazel twig."

Giddy-up, Horsey

Giddy-up, horsey, off we go,
Clippety cloppety, nice and slow.
Clippety, cloppety, down the lane,
All the way, then back again.

Feathers

Cackle, cackle, Mother Goose,
Have you any feathers loose?
"Truly have I, pretty fellow,
Half enough to fill a pillow.
Here are quills, take one or two,
And down to make a bed for you."

A Green Frog

Said the little green frog,
As he sat on a log,
"Nobody really likes me."
A duck came along,
And said, "You are wrong"
And gobbled him up for tea.

An Elephant Walks

An elephant walks like this and that;
He's terribly tall and he's terribly fat.
He's got no fingers,
He's got no toes,
But goodness gracious
What a long, long nose!

Mermaid's Treasure

One morning, Pearl the mermaid was playing around a reef when she spotted a large sea chest among the coral. She swam closer.

"It must have fallen out of a ship," she exclaimed. "I wonder what's inside!"

But when she tried to lift the lid, she found that it was locked.

"Oh, bother," Pearl muttered. "Now I want to look inside even more!"

She tried to force the lid open with a clamshell, but it wouldn't budge. So she asked her biggest, strongest friends for help.

Shark tried to bite a hole in it. Octopus wrapped his tentacles around the chest and tried to squeeze it open. Whale tried crushing it with his weight.

"It's no use," sighed Pearl. "We'll never get it open."

"May I try?" said a squeaky voice in her ear.

Pearl turned and saw a tiny shrimp, no bigger than her fingernail. She smiled at him. How could someone so small open the chest?

"Of course you may," she said politely.

The little shrimp wriggled through the keyhole. Pearl, Shark, Octopus, and Whale watched as he reached into the lock with his spindly legs. Then there was a loud click, and the chest unlocked.

The shrimp swam out, looking very pleased with himself.

"Well done!" cried Pearl.

Slowly, she lifted the lid. The chest was full of men's clothes! Pearl sat back and laughed loudly.

"Some poor sailor has lost his luggage," she chuckled. "I suppose it would be treasure to him!"

She looked at her friends and laughed again.

"Don't look so disappointed," she went on. "We may not have gold or jewels, but we've made a very clever friend."

And the little pink shrimp blushed bright red!

For Want of a Nail

For want of a nail, the shoe was lost;
For want of the shoe, the horse was lost;
For want of the horse, the rider was lost;
For want of the rider, the battle was lost;
For want of the battle, the kingdom was lost;
And all from the want of a horseshoe nail.

Peas Porridge

Peas porridge hot,
Peas porridge cold,
Peas porridge in the pot,
Nine days old.
Some like it hot,
Some like it cold,
Some like it in the pot,
Nine days old.

Jack Sprat

Jack Sprat could eat no fat,
His wife could eat no lean,
And so between the two of them
They licked the platter clean.

I Scream

I scream, you scream,
We all scream for ice cream!

Old Joe Brown

Old Joe Brown, he had a wife,
She was all of eight feet tall.
She slept with her head in the kitchen,
And her feet stuck out in the hall.

I Met a Man

As I was going up the stair
I met a man who wasn't there.
He wasn't there again today—
Oh! How I wish he'd go away!

The Littlest Pig

Little Pig had a secret. He snuggled down in the warm hay with his family and smiled a secret smile. Maybe it wasn't so bad being the littlest pig after all …

Not so long ago, Little Pig had been feeling really fed up. He was the smallest pig in the family. He had five brothers and five sisters and they were all much bigger and fatter than he was. They were very greedy and ate most of the food from the feeding trough before Little Pig had a chance!

Then one day Little Pig had made an important discovery: a little hole in the fence, tucked away behind the feeding trough. He could just fit through the hole because he was so little.

He waited all day until it was time for bed, and then, when all his family were fast asleep, he wriggled through the hole. Suddenly he was outside, free to go wherever he pleased. And what an adventure he had!

First, he ran to the henhouse and gobbled up the bowls of grain. Then he ran into the vegetable patch and munched a whole row of cabbages. What a wonderful feast! When his little belly was full to bursting, he headed for home.

Night after night Little Pig had tasty adventures. Sometimes he would find the farm dog's bowl filled with scraps from the farmer's supper, or come across buckets of oats ready for the horses.

As the days and weeks went by, Little Pig grew bigger and fatter. He knew that soon he would no longer be able to fit through the hole, but for now, snuggled down in the warm hay, he was enjoying his secret!

Five Little
Speckled Frogs

Five little speckled frogs,
Sat on a speckled log,
Eating the most delicious bugs,
Yum, yum!
One jumped into the pool,
Where it was nice and cool.
Now there are four green speckled frogs,
Glub, glub!

*(Repeat the rhyme, counting down from five little
speckled frogs to one little speckled frog …)*

One little speckled frog,
Sat on a speckled log,
Eating the most delicious bugs,
Yum, yum!
He jumped into the pool,
Where it was nice and cool.
Now there are no green speckled frogs,
Glub, glub!

Long-Legged Sailor

Have you ever, ever, ever,
in your long-legged life
met a long-legged sailor
with a long-legged wife?
No, I never, never, never,
in my long-legged life
met a long-legged sailor
with a long-legged wife!

Rub a Dub Dub

Rub a dub dub,
Three men in a tub,
And how do you think they got there?
The butcher, the baker,
The candlestick maker,
And all of them gone to the fair.

The Pink Princess

Princess Sophia loved pink. She had a bright pink room—with a plump pink bed. She had a huge pink wardrobe full of frilly pink dresses. She had rosebud-pink shoes and a pink tiara.

One day, Princess Chloe came to play at the palace. She brought Princess Sophia a lovely new necklace! But there was only one problem …

"It's not pink!" cried Princess Sophia. It really was beautiful, but it wouldn't go with her pink dress, pink shoes, or pink tiara!

"Let's go and play!" cried Princess Chloe.

Princess Sophia put the necklace in her pocket and followed Princess Chloe into the palace garden.

Princess Chloe ran up to the gardener, who was busy mowing the palace lawn.

"May we pick some flowers, please?" asked Princess Chloe.

When the gardener said that they could, Princess Chloe skipped away, picking different-colored flowers as she went.

Princess Sophia noticed some bright purple blossom. She picked some of it and put it in her hair, just like Princess Chloe.

Princess Chloe started to climb a huge tree.

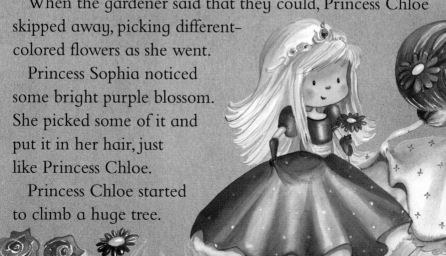

"Princesses don't climb trees!" gasped Princess Sophia.

"Why not?" said Princess Chloe. "Look, I've found some ribbons up here!"

Princess Sophia recognized the ribbons of a kite she had lost. She climbed up into the tree. Princess Chloe untangled the ribbons and tied one around each of their waists.

"Now catch me if you can!" said Princess Chloe, and she scrambled down the tree and ran to the pond.

A dragonfly fluttered past them, its shimmering wings catching the sun. It landed on Princess Chloe's outstretched hand. Princess Sophia jumped back nervously.

Princess Chloe whispered to the dragonfly, "She doesn't like anything that isn't pink."

"Yes, I do!" shouted Princess Sophia. "I like the bright flowers and the rainbow-colored ribbons, and the blue pond and this gorgeous, multi-colored dragonfly!"

"Why don't you try on your new necklace now?" asked Princess Chloe.

Princess Sophia admired her colorful reflection in the pond.

"I don't mind that it's not a pink necklace ..." she said, smiling. "Because I'm not just a pink princess any more!"

Come to Bed, Says Sleepy-Head

"Come to bed," says Sleepy-head,
"Tarry a while," says Slow,
"Put on the pot," says Greedy-gut,
"Let's sup before we go."

Wee Willie Winkie

Wee Willie Winkie
Runs through the town,
Upstairs and downstairs
In his nightgown.
Rapping at the window,
Crying through the lock,
"Are the children all in bed?
It's past eight o'clock."

Brahms' Lullaby

Lullaby, and good night,
With rosy bed light,
With lilies overspread,
Is my sweet baby's head.
Lay you down now and rest,
May your slumber be blessed.
Lay you down now and rest,
May your slumber be blessed.

Go to Sleep

Go to sleep, my baby,
Close your pretty eyes,
Angels are above us,
Peeping through the skies.
Great big moon is shining,
Stars begin to peep.
Time for little babies
All to go to sleep.

Diddle Diddle Dumpling

Diddle, diddle, dumpling, my son John,
Went to bed with his trousers on,
One shoe off, and one shoe on,
Diddle, diddle, dumpling, my son John.

The Owl and the Pussy Cat

The Owl and the Pussy Cat went to sea
In a beautiful pea-green boat,
They took some honey, and plenty of money,
Wrapped up in a five-pound note.

The Owl looked up to the stars above,
And sang to a small guitar,
"Oh lovely Pussy Cat! Oh Pussy Cat, my love,
What a beautiful Pussy Cat you are, you are,
What a beautiful Pussy Cat you are."

Pussy Cat said to the Owl, "You elegant fowl,
How charmingly sweet you sing.
Oh let us be married, too long we have tarried.
But what shall we do for a ring?"

They sailed away, for a year and a day,
To the land where the Bong-tree grows,
And there in a wood a Piggy-wig stood
With a ring at the end of his nose, his nose, his nose,
With a ring at the end of his nose.

The Snow Queen

Once, there was a wicked imp who made a magic mirror. Everything it reflected looked ugly and mean. One day, the mirror smashed into tiny specks, and the specks got into people's eyes and made everything look bad to them. Some specks became caught in people's hearts, making them feel grumpy.

A few of the specks from the mirror floated toward a far-away place, where there lived two best friends, named Gerda and Kay.

The pair spent endless days together. In the winter, Gerda's grandmother told them wonderful stories while the snow swirled outside.

"The Snow Queen brings the winter weather," she would say. "She peeps in at the windows and leaves icy patterns on the glass."

In the summer, the children would play in the little roof garden between their houses. One sunny day, they were reading together when Kay let out a cry. Specks from the imp's magic mirror had caught in Kay's eye and his heart.

Kay became bad-tempered throughout the summer and the autumn and was still cross when winter came. One snowy day, he stormed off with his sled. Suddenly, a large white sleigh swept past, and Kay mischievously hitched his sled to the back.

The sleigh pulled him far, far away. When it finally stopped, Kay realized the sleigh belonged to the Snow Queen from Gerda's grandmother's story! She kissed Kay's forehead, and her icy touch froze his heart. He forgot all about Gerda and his home.

Back home, Gerda missed Kay. She searched everywhere for him. Just as she was about to give up, Gerda noticed a little boat among the rushes down by the river.

"Perhaps the river will carry me to Kay," she thought. She climbed in, and the boat glided away.

Many hours later, the boat reached the shore. A large raven came hopping toward Gerda.

"I think I have seen your friend," the raven croaked. "A young man who sounds like him has married a princess. I'll take you there."

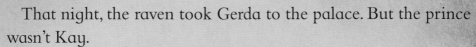

That night, the raven took Gerda to the palace. But the prince wasn't Kay.

Poor Gerda! She was far from home. She told the prince and princess her story. They promised to help her, and the next morning Gerda was given warm clothes and a golden sleigh.

She set off into the woods, but before long she was spotted by a band of robbers.

"That carriage is pure gold!" they hissed.

The robbers sprang out and captured Gerda. Suddenly the daughter of the robber chief appeared. The girl was lonely and excited by the thought of a new friend.

"Please, treat her gently!" the robber girl pleaded. "She can stay with me."

Gerda was grateful to the robber girl for her kindness.

Inside the robber's den, Gerda met the robber girl's pet reindeer. When Gerda told her new friend about Kay, the reindeer spoke, saying he had seen Kay with the Snow Queen.

"I know the way to the Snow Queen's palace," added the reindeer. "I will take you there."

It was a long, cold journey, but at last Gerda and the reindeer arrived outside the Snow Queen's palace.

Inside the ice palace, the Snow Queen still held Kay under her spell.

"Spring is coming," she announced suddenly. "I must leave. It is time for me to make it snow on the other side of the world!" And she flew off in her sleigh, leaving Kay alone.

At that moment, Gerda crept into the palace. When she saw her friend, she wept. Her tears fell onto his chest. They melted his cold heart and washed away the speck of glass. Kay began to cry too, and his tears washed the glass from his eye. At last he was free from the spell!

The reindeer carried Gerda and Kay back home.

"Grandmother!" called Gerda. "We're back at last!"

The old lady was so happy to see them, and she hugged them tightly.

"I knew that you would come home one day," she cried. "Now, tell me all about your adventures!"

Thirty Days Hath September

Thirty days hath September, April, June, and November.
All the rest have thirty-one,
Except February alone,
And that has twenty-eight days clear
And twenty-nine in each leap year.

The Farmer in the Dell

The farmer in the dell,
The farmer in the dell,
Hi-ho, the derry-o,
The farmer in the dell.

This Old Man

This old man, he played one,
He played knick-knack on my drum.
With a knick-knack, paddy whack,
Give a dog a bone,
This old man came rolling home.

Repeat the rhyme, replacing 'one' and 'drum' with:
two—shoe, three—knee, four—door, five—hive,
six—sticks, seven—heaven, eight—gate.

Higglety, Pigglety, Pop!

Higglety, pigglety, pop!
The dog has eaten the mop,
The pig's in a hurry,
The cat's in a flurry,
Higglety, pigglety, POP!

My Favorite Chair

My favorite chair is small like me,
I sit on it to watch TV.
And sometimes when I read a book
I take my chair into a nook
And sit there while I turn the pages,
I often stay like that for ages.

Here Is the Church

Here is the church,
Here is the steeple,
Look inside …
And see all the people!

Elsie's Playhouse

One hot summer's day, Elsie found her dad snoozing in his deckchair.

"Dad," she called out. "I'd really like a playhouse in the backyard. Will you build me one?"

"Of course, Elsie, anything you like," Dad replied, dozily. Then he turned over and fell right back to sleep.

Elsie smiled and skipped happily away. She couldn't wait to play in her new playhouse!

"Is the playhouse finished, Dad?" Elsie asked an hour later.

Dad was still lying in his deckchair. "Elsie, making a playhouse is not as easy as all that!" he explained. "First, we'll have to draw a plan, and then …"

"That's OK, Dad. I know exactly how I want it," said Elsie. "Look, I've drawn a picture."

Elsie's playhouse had pink walls, four little windows, and a bright red front door.

"Oh, I see," sighed Dad, "but I'll have to find some wood first …"

"That's okay, Dad," giggled Elsie. "There are pieces of wood in the shed."

After an hour, they had collected enough wood to make the playhouse. Dad was very hot, dusty, and covered with cobwebs.

"So, can you start building it now, Dad?" asked Elsie.

"Ah, well, um, I'll need to find my tools …" groaned Dad.

"Don't worry, Dad, I've found them for you," grinned Elsie, giving him the toolbox.

Dad laughed. "Thank you. I suppose I can't put this off any longer!"

So, for the rest of the afternoon, until darkness fell, Dad hammered, drilled, sawed, and painted, until … he finished the playhouse. It looked just like Elsie's drawing.

"Elsie will be so pleased," thought Dad, exhausted. He couldn't wait to see the look on her face.

But when he went into the living room, Elsie was fast asleep on the sofa.

"Elsie," he called gently. "Wake up, your playhouse is finished!"

"Thanks, Dad," Elsie whispered, "I'll play in it tomorrow." And she fell right back to sleep!

Best Friends' Christmas

Sarah and Rosina were best friends, and when they wrote their Christmas lists, they both asked for exactly the same thing: "A baby doll to play with, and one for my best friend too."

Not far away, in the toy factory, the toymakers were working hard to get ready for Christmas. They made piles of teddies and board games and baby dolls, and loaded them into sacks for Santa Claus to deliver. One morning, they got a surprise.

"Look at this!" said one of the toymakers, pointing at the dolls. "These two have made friends!"

Two baby dolls named Janey and Lucy were holding hands. The toymakers smiled, then pulled their hands away from each other and put them into different sacks. They didn't notice how sad the dolls looked.

On Christmas morning, Rosina unwrapped a big box and found Janey inside.

"I love her," said Rosina, cuddling Janey. "But she looks a bit sad."

She ran to Sarah's house at the end of the street, and Sarah came running out to meet her. She was holding a baby doll that looked a bit sad too.

"This is Lucy," Sarah said.

Janey and Lucy were delighted to see each other again and their sad expressions changed. Rosina suddenly realized that the little dolls looked happy and were gazing at each other with sparkly eyes.

"I get the feeling that these two are going to be best friends, just like us," she said to Sarah.

"Perhaps they already are," said Sarah wisely.

Fairy Friends Forever

Deep in the woods, poor Eloise the fairy was trapped under a nutshell that had fallen from a tree. Try as she might, it was just too heavy for her to move.

Then suddenly the nutshell lifted, and a little girl gazed down at her.

Eloise was scared of humans, but the girl looked kind.

"Thank you," she said. "What's your name?"

"Matilda," whispered the girl. "Are you really a fairy?"

Suddenly Eloise had an idea. She waved her wand and shrank Matilda to fairy size.

"Come to Fairyland and find out!" she giggled.

Eloise showed Matilda all around her magical home. They had tea in her toadstool house and gathered dewberries in the Fairyland Forest. They giggled and shared secrets, and soon they felt as if they had always known each other.

Then it was time for Matilda to go home. Eloise gave her a tiny Fairyland flower.

"I'll never forget you," she whispered.

"And I won't forget you," promised Matilda, as they linked their little fingers together. "Fairy friends forever!"

Winter Snowdrops

One winter's day, a fairy named Snowdrop was sitting in a tree when she heard someone crying. She fluttered down and saw a girl sitting among the tree roots.

"What's wrong, little girl?" Snowdrop asked.

"I can't find any flowers for my mother's birthday," sobbed the girl.

Snowdrop felt sorry for her.

"Fetch me the smoothest pebble you can find," she said. "Then bury it under the tree."

The little girl searched and searched, and finally found a pebble as smooth as silk. She buried it as she'd been told, and patted the soil down. Then Snowdrop waved her wand, and tiny plant shoots poked through the soil and started to grow. They rose higher and higher, until they burst into brilliant white snowdrops.

"Thank you!" said the little girl, picking the flowers. "Mommy will love them."

The little girl never saw Snowdrop again. But every year, on the girl's mother's birthday, Snowdrop secretly used her magic, and there was always a patch of bright snowdrops waiting for her to pick them!

Baby in a Cradle

The baby in the cradle
Goes rock-a-rock-a-rock.
The clock on the dresser
Goes tick-a-tick-a-tock.
The rain on the window
Goes tap-a-tap-a-tap,
But here comes the sun,
So we clap-a-clap-a-clap!

Rock-a-Bye, Baby

Rock-a-bye, baby, in the tree top,
When the wind blows, the cradle will rock.
When the bough breaks, the cradle will fall,
And down will come baby, cradle and all.

I See the Moon

I see the moon and the moon sees me.
God bless the moon, and God bless me.

Little Fred

When little Fred went to bed,
He always said his prayers,
He kissed Mama, and then Papa,
And straightaway went upstairs.

Go to Bed, Tom

Go to bed, Tom,
Go to bed, Tom,
Tired or not, Tom,
Go to bed, Tom.

Bend and Stretch

Bend and stretch, reach for the stars.
There goes Jupiter, here comes Mars.
Bend and stretch, reach for the sky.
Stand on tip-e-toe, oh! So high!

353

Princess Ava and the Big Smile

Princess Ava was a very lively girl. She was always bouncing around and getting into scrapes. But her father wanted her to act more like a princess.

"You need to be more serious," the king told his daughter.

The princess looked at the king's serious face. And then she looked at his down-turned mouth. He looked very sad, so she put her arms around him and gave him a kiss.

"It's not me who needs to be more serious," she told the king, "it's you who needs to smile more, Daddy."

Princess Ava showed the king how to dance around the palace gardens and do cartwheels. The king wasn't very good at them, but he kept on trying, and suddenly, his face wasn't quite so serious.

Princess Ava showed the king how to make a kite swoop through the sky like a bird. The king kept getting his string tangled, but his face was looking less serious by the minute.

"Well done, Daddy!" cried Princess Ava. The king's mouth twitched. It started to turn up at the corners. Then he gave Ava the most wonderful smile.

"I had forgotten how much fun it is to do cartwheels and fly kites," he laughed.

"Oh, Daddy, you do look silly!" giggled Princess Ava.

The happy king did a cartwheel and bounced onto his throne. He was going to pass some new laws in his kingdom.

"From now on," said the king, "I decree that everyone must do at least ten cartwheels a day. And everyone in the palace will have one hour off every morning to practice kite flying."

The king gave Princess Ava a beautiful charm necklace.

"This will remind you that everyone needs a little bit of silliness and fun to keep them smiling," he said.

"Oh, Daddy," giggled Princess Ava, "I've always known that!" And she danced out of the palace to play.

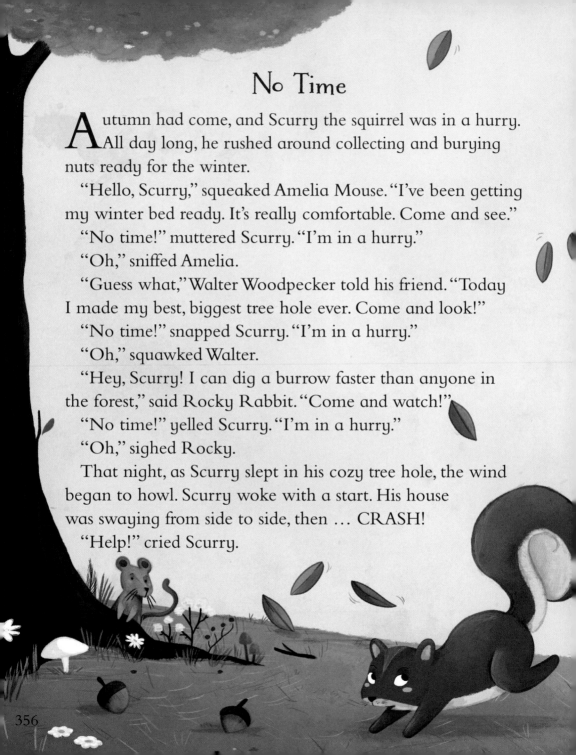

No Time

Autumn had come, and Scurry the squirrel was in a hurry. All day long, he rushed around collecting and burying nuts ready for the winter.

"Hello, Scurry," squeaked Amelia Mouse. "I've been getting my winter bed ready. It's really comfortable. Come and see."

"No time!" muttered Scurry. "I'm in a hurry."

"Oh," sniffed Amelia.

"Guess what," Walter Woodpecker told his friend. "Today I made my best, biggest tree hole ever. Come and look!"

"No time!" snapped Scurry. "I'm in a hurry."

"Oh," squawked Walter.

"Hey, Scurry! I can dig a burrow faster than anyone in the forest," said Rocky Rabbit. "Come and watch!"

"No time!" yelled Scurry. "I'm in a hurry."

"Oh," sighed Rocky.

That night, as Scurry slept in his cozy tree hole, the wind began to howl. Scurry woke with a start. His house was swaying from side to side, then … CRASH!

"Help!" cried Scurry.

"What's the matter?" called Amelia from her bed.

"My tree's blown over," whimpered Scurry. "Where am I going to sleep?"

"Come and share my warm bed," said Amelia. "There's plenty of space."

"Thank you," said Scurry, quietly.

The next morning, Scurry wept when he saw his damaged home.

"Where will I find a comfortable tree hole like that again?" he cried to his friends.

"Easy!" said Walter. "I told you I'd made a great hole. It'll be perfect for you."

"Thank you," said Scurry, quietly. "But how am I going to move all the nuts? My tree has fallen on top of them."

"No problem," said Rocky. "I can dig them out for you."

When all the hard work was over, Scurry called his friends together.

"Come and have supper in my new home," he said, "as a thank you for helping me."

"No time!" said his friends. "We're in a hurry."

Scurry hung his head. Then the three friends burst out laughing.

"Oh, Scurry," they said. "We always have time for a friend!"

Sparrow

Little brown sparrow, sat upon a tree,
Way up in the branches, safe as he can be!
Hopping through the green leaves, he will play,
High above the ground is where he will stay.

Little Ginger Cat

Little ginger cat,
Sitting in the sun,
Watching all the birds
Flying just for fun.
Hear them chirp and tweet,
As they fly so free,
Just as if to say,
"You cannot catch me!"

Little Robin Redbreast

Little Robin Redbreast
Sat upon a rail:
Niddle-noddle went his head!
Wiggle-waggle went his tail.

The North Wind Doth Blow

The north wind doth blow,
And we shall have snow,
And what will poor Robin do then?
Poor thing!

He'll sit in a barn,
And to keep himself warm,
Will hide his head under his wing.
Poor thing!

Magpies

One for sorrow, two for joy,
Three for a girl, four for a boy,
Five for silver, six for gold,
Seven for a secret never to be told.

Run, Little Mice

Run, little mice, little mice run!
Don't let that naughty cat have his fun.
Hide beneath the floor until he's gone away,
And then, little mice, come on out and play!

359

Rapunzel

Once upon a time, a poor young couple lived in a cottage next door to an old witch. The witch grew many vegetables in her garden, but she kept them all for herself.

One day the couple had only a few potatoes left to eat.

"Surely it wouldn't matter if we took just a few vegetables," said the wife, gazing longingly over the wall.

So her husband quickly climbed into the garden and started to fill his basket. Suddenly he heard an angry voice.

"How dare you steal my vegetables!"

"Please don't hurt me," begged the young man. "My wife is going to have a baby soon!"

"You may keep the vegetables," she croaked. "But you must give me the baby when it is born." Terrified, the man had to agree.

Months later, the woman gave birth to a little girl. And although the parents begged and cried, the cruel witch took the baby. She called her Rapunzel.

Years passed, and Rapunzel grew up to be kind and beautiful. The witch was so afraid of losing her that she built a tall tower with no door and only one window. She planted thorn bushes all around it, then she locked Rapunzel in the tower.

Each day, Rapunzel brushed and combed her long, golden locks.

And each day the witch came to visit her, standing at the foot of the tower and calling out, "Rapunzel, Rapunzel, let down your hair."

Rapunzel hung her hair out of the window, and the witch climbed up it to sit and talk with her. But Rapunzel was very lonely. Each day, she sat at her window and sang sadly.

One day, a prince rode by and heard the beautiful singing coming from the witch's garden. As he hid behind the wall, he saw the old witch call out, "Rapunzel, Rapunzel, let down your hair."

The prince saw a cascade of golden hair fall from the tower, and he watched the witch climb up it.

When the witch returned to her house, he crept to the tower. "Rapunzel, Rapunzel, let down your hair," he called softly.

Rapunzel let down her locks, and the prince climbed up.

Rapunzel was very surprised to see the prince, and delighted when he said he wanted to be her friend. From then on, the prince came to visit her every day.

Months passed, and Rapunzel and the prince fell in love.

"How can we be together?" Rapunzel cried. "The witch will never let me go."

So the prince brought some silk, which Rapunzel knotted together to make a ladder so that she could escape from the tower.

One day, without thinking, Rapunzel remarked to the witch, "It's much harder to pull you up than the prince!"

The witch was furious! "What prince?" she shouted.

She grabbed Rapunzel's long hair and cut it off. Then she used her magic to send Rapunzel far into the forest.

That evening, when the prince came to see Rapunzel, the witch held the golden hair out of the window, and he climbed up into the tower, coming face to face with the old witch.

"You will never see Rapunzel again!" she screamed, and pushed the prince out of the window. He fell into the thorn bushes below. The sharp spikes scratched his eyes and blinded him. Weeping, he stumbled away.

After months of wandering, blind and lost, the prince heard beautiful, sad singing floating through the woods. He recognized Rapunzel's voice and called out to her.

"At last I have found you!" she cried. As her tears fell onto the prince's eyes, his wounds healed, and he could see again.

Rapunzel had never been so happy. She and the prince were soon married, and they lived happily ever after, far away from the old witch and her empty tower.

Not-So-Scary

Glob the monster longed to be big and scary, but he had never frightened anyone. He had never even made anyone jump.

"I'm just too nice," he thought to himself. "Monsters aren't supposed to be friendly!"

One day at monster school, Glob saw a purple monster with yellow spots, called Murkle. Glob jumped out from behind a wall to try to scare her. ROAR! He was pleased to see she was crying.

"Are you crying because I scared you?" asked Glob.

Murkle shook her head.

"I'm crying because I've got no one to share my sweets with," she said.

"Oh," said Glob, disappointed. "I've never tried sweets before."

Murkle held out the bag with a big monster smile.

"Try one," she said.

Together, Glob and Murkle munched up the whole bag. By the time they had finished the last one, they were best friends. They both decided never to scare anyone again.

"Sweets are delicious!" said Glob. "And I think being friendly is better than being scary."

Monster Nursery School

Monster nursery school is a lot like normal nursery school. There are teachers and toys and books. But of course, not everything is the same.

At monster nursery school, you have to be NOISY! The teachers tell you off for walking, as you're supposed to run everywhere. If you make a big mess when you eat then you'd fit right in at monster nursery school.

Every morning, the little monsters sing a special song.

"Naughty monsters just like me
Love to shout and sing!
Let's all make a dreadful mess
And jump on everything!"

Then they practice making rude noises and bouncing on cushions.

In the afternoon, the little monsters do painting, just like you. But they don't paint on paper. They paint on each other!

I'm afraid only little monsters are allowed to go to monster nursery school, so you will just have to read about it here instead. Unless, of course, you're a little monster too!

Go to Bed Late

Go to bed late,
Stay very small.
Go to bed early,
Grow very tall.

Go to Bed First

Go to bed first,
A golden purse,
Go to bed second,
A golden pheasant,
Go to bed third,
A golden bird.

Sleep, Little Child

Sleep, little child, go to sleep,
Mother is here by your bed.
Sleep, little child, go to sleep,
Rest on the pillow your head.
The world is silent and still,
The moon shines bright on the hill,
Then creeps past the window sill.
Oh sleep, go to sleep.

Hush, Little Baby

Hush, little baby, don't say a word,
Papa's gonna buy you a mockingbird.

If that mockingbird don't sing,
Papa's gonna buy you a diamond ring.

If that diamond ring turns to brass,
Papa's gonna buy you a looking-glass.

If that looking-glass gets broke,
Papa's gonna buy you a billy goat.

If that billy goat don't pull,
Papa's gonna buy you a cart and mule.

If that cart and mule turn over,
Papa's gonna buy you a dog named Rover.

If that dog named Rover won't bark,
Papa's gonna buy you a horse and cart.

If that horse and cart fall down,
You'll still be the sweetest little baby in town.

The Little Wolf with a Big Boast

Little Wolf was always boasting. "I'm so clever, I could give the teachers lessons," he said. "And I'm so funny, if I told a joke you'd probably laugh for three days without stopping."

Little Wolf's parents told him not to boast, but he didn't listen. One day he started to talk about the weather.

"I'm so fierce, I bet even the weather is scared of me," he said one evening.

Unluckily for Little Wolf, the weather was listening.

"Hmm," said the weather. "I think someone needs to teach this little wolf a lesson!"

When Little Wolf went out to play, the weather followed him. First it rained so heavily that his coat was drenched.

"I need some shelter," said Little Wolf.

He crept under a low rock and curled up to wait for the rain to stop. But as soon as it did, the weather grew hotter … and hotter … and hotter.

"I can't curl up here any longer," panted Little Wolf. "I need a nice cool swim."

He ran to the stream and dived in.

So the weather blew wind so hard that big waves crashed down on Little Wolf's head. He pulled himself out of the water just as snow began to fall. Shivering, he ran the rest of the way home. His parents were curled up inside their cozy cave, and Little Wolf snuggled up to them.

"I've been very silly," he whispered.

He told them what he had said about the weather, and his mother kissed his furry head.

"Now the weather has had its fun, I'm sure it has forgiven you," she said sleepily.

Little Wolf smiled as he closed his eyes. Perhaps, if he promised not to boast any more, the weather would play with him tomorrow … but nicely this time!

The Curious Star

Once upon a time there was a curious star that wanted to know what humans were really like. So, one night, he let go of the sky and fell all the way down to Earth. When he landed, he plopped into a muddy puddle next to a pigsty.

"Hello," said the star to a round, pink creature. "Are you a human?"

"No," chuckled the pig. "Humans are much taller than me!"

So the star went shooting through the sky until he spotted a tall creature with a very long neck.

"Hello," said the star. "Are you a human?"

"No," smiled the giraffe. "Humans only have two legs. I have four."

The star sighed. He was longing to meet a real human. He zoomed on until he spotted someone standing on two legs and squawking.

"Hello," said the star. "Are you a human?"

"Certainly not!" said the parrot. "Humans aren't as bright and beautiful as I am!"

"Oh dear," said the star. "Perhaps I'll never meet a human."

When the sun came up, he flew down to a sandy beach to rest. Before long, a creature with curious eyes and messy hair kneeled down beside him.

"Hello," said the star. "Are you a human?"

"Yes, I am," laughed the little boy. "My name's Noah. Would you like to play with me?"

The star jumped up in excitement. Together they explored rock pools, made sandcastles, and played hide and seek all day. And the star found out that Noah was very, very curious—just like him!

When night fell, the curious star said goodbye to Noah.

"Don't stop being curious," he said. "Exploring new things can take you to amazing places."

With a blast of silver light, the star shot into the air and took his place again in the twinkling night sky.

Jack and Jill

Jack and Jill went up the hill
To fetch a pail of water;
Jack fell down and broke his crown,
And Jill came tumbling after.
Up Jack got, and home did trot
As fast as he could caper;
He went to bed, to mend his head,
With vinegar and brown paper.

Rain, Rain, Go Away

Rain, rain, go away,
Come again another day.
Rain, rain, go away,
Little Johnny wants to play.

Doctor Foster

Doctor Foster
Went to Gloucester
In a shower of rain.
He stepped in a puddle,
Right up to his middle,
And never went there again!

It's Raining, It's Pouring

It's raining, it's pouring,
The old man is snoring.
He went to bed and bumped his head,
And couldn't get up in the morning.

I Hear Thunder

I hear thunder, I hear thunder.
Oh, don't you? Oh, don't you?
Pitter, patter, raindrops,
Pitter, patter, raindrops.
I'm wet through! So are you!

Bobby Shaftoe's Gone to Sea

Bobby Shaftoe's gone to sea,
Silver buckles at his knee;
He'll come back and marry me,
Bonny Bobby Shaftoe!

Three Little Ghosties

Three little ghosties,
Sitting on posties,
Eating buttered toasties,
Munching and slurping,
With lots of burping!
Oh, what beasties,
To make such feasties!

What Ghosts Like Best

The friendliest ghost in the fairground was named Milo, and he loved telling jokes.

"Do humans like jokes?" he asked the other ghosts.

"Don't ask silly questions," they said. "Humans hate jokes."

One day, a sad-looking boy named William got on the ghost train. Milo sat next to him.

"Hello," he said. "Do you like jokes?"

William looked scared, but Milo thought he'd try a joke anyway.

"What do ghosts eat?" Milo asked. "Spook-hetti!"

He felt pleased when William giggled.

"What do you call a train with a cold?" he went on. "Achoo choo train!"

William giggled again. All the way around the ride, Milo told jokes and William laughed.

"Is it okay if I come back tomorrow?" asked William at the end of the ride. "I've never laughed so much in my life!"

Milo grinned. "Of course," he said. "And now I know that humans definitely do like jokes!"

Surprise at the Shops

When Benjamin Mouse saw a blue bike in the toyshop window, Mr. Mouse said bikes were silly. Benjamin thought his daddy was a bit too serious.

"Help me do the shopping instead," Mr. Mouse said.

"Shopping is boring," grumbled Benjamin.

"Perhaps it'll be more fun than you think," said Mr. Mouse.

At the grocer's, Mr. Mouse picked out some carrots and some apples. Out of the corner of his eye, Benjamin saw the grocer juggle some apples and oranges. He told his daddy, who frowned.

"Grocers are too sensible to juggle," he said.

At the dairy, while Mr. Mouse collected some milk and cheese, Benjamin saw Mrs. Cow twirling in a pink tutu. He told his daddy, who shook his head.

"Cows are far too busy to dance," he said.

The final stop was the bakery. While Mr. Mouse was busy choosing some rolls and buns for tea, Benjamin saw the baker balancing fifteen doughnuts on the tip of her nose. Benjamin told his daddy, who sighed.

"You're imagining things," he said. "Bakers don't play with their food."

As they passed the toyshop on the way home, the door opened and the toymaker wheeled out the blue bike.

"Oh, no," gasped Benjamin. "It's been sold!"

"Yes, it has," said the toymaker. "It belongs to YOU!"

Benjamin stared at his daddy in amazement.

"Did you buy it?" he asked.

"Me?" Mr. Mouse said. "I'm far too serious to buy toys!"

But he exchanged a secret wink with the toymaker as Benjamin jumped onto the bike in excitement.

"I'll help with the shopping again tomorrow," Benjamin promised. "You were right—it's much more fun than I thought!"

The Princess and the Pea

Once upon a time, there lived a handsome prince. He had loving parents, plenty of friends, and lived a wonderful life in his castle. But one thing made him sad. He did not have a wife.

The prince had always wanted to marry a princess. But he wanted her to be clever and funny, and loving and kind. None of the princesses that he met at parties and balls was quite right.

Some of the princesses were too mean, some were too rude.

Some were too quiet, some were too loud.

And some were just plain boring!

So the prince decided to travel the world in the hope of finding a perfect princess. He met many more princesses who tried to impress him with their beauty, their dancing, and their baking … but still none was quite right.

"I'm never going to meet the girl of my dreams," he sighed to himself.

"Cheer up, son," said the king. "You are still young. One day you will meet a wonderful girl, just like I met your mother."

Several months later, when even the king and queen had begun to give up hope of their son ever finding a bride, there was a terrible storm. Suddenly there was a loud knock on the castle door.

"I wonder who could be out on such a terrible stormy night?" said the prince. When he opened the door, a pretty young girl stared back at him. She was soaked from head to toe.

"Please may I come in for a moment?" she pleaded. "I was traveling to see some friends, but I got lost in this storm, and now I am very cold and wet."

"You poor thing," said the queen. "You must stay the night. You cannot travel on in this weather."

The prince smiled at the girl. "What is your name?"

"I'm Princess Penelope," she replied. "You are all very kind. I don't want to be a bother to you."

At the word "princess," the queen smiled to herself. She took the girl's hand and said, "Of course not. Let's get you warm and dry."

Later, the prince listened contentedly as the charming princess chatted away over supper. She was clever and funny, and loving and kind. By the end of the evening he'd fallen in love!

The queen was delighted when she saw what was happening, but she wanted to be quite sure that Penelope was a real princess.

She went to the guest room in the castle and placed a tiny pea under the mattress. Then she told the servants to pile twenty more mattresses onto the bed, and then twenty feather quilts on top of the twenty mattresses!

The queen showed the princess to her room. "Sleep well, my dear," she said.

In the morning the queen asked Penelope how she'd slept.

Penelope didn't want to be rude, but she couldn't lie. "I'm afraid I hardly slept a wink!" she replied.

"I'm so sorry," replied the queen. "Was the bed not comfortable?"

"There were so many lovely mattresses and quilts, it should have been very comfortable," replied the princess, "but I could feel something lumpy, and now I am black and blue all over!"

The queen grinned and hugged the girl to her. "That proves it," she cried. "Only a real princess would be able to feel a tiny pea through twenty mattresses and twenty feather quilts!"

The prince was filled with joy. He had finally met the princess of his dreams!

Not long after that, the prince asked Princess Penelope to be his wife. They married, and the prince was never unhappy again. And as for the pea, it was put in the royal museum as proof that perfect princesses do exist!

Index

384